Timothy Patrick Means

DEAR SOMEONE

Mad Dog Publications

I would like to dedicate this book to my sister, Peggie, who, from the beginning, was the first who supported me by purchasing my book. Plus, the question I enjoy hearing most is, How do you think up this stuff?

Chapter 1

Lillian Newburg, a hard-working single girl in her mid-twenties, finished putting away the last files of a client's mortgage paperwork. It was a Friday afternoon; she was anxious to get home. That evening she was to meet on a blind date arranged by her close friend Amy.

When she reached her car parked off the busy boulevard, she noticed something unusual sitting under the windshield wiper: a gold-colored card, no bigger than a postcard. Removing the card, she saw that it was addressed to *Dear Someone.* Thinking this was odd, perhaps a practical joke, she turned around to see if anyone was watching her.

Holding the small envelope in her hand, she quickly tore it open; inside was a black card with something strange written in gold letters.

Dear Someone,
You don't know me, and you probably think this strange. Regardless of your opinions, the outcome will be the same. Be aware and watch for the things that go bump. These violent delights have violent ends.
Signed,
Concerned

Lillian looked around her, expecting someone to jump out to grab her. Her heart raced as if blood was escaping her body.

Slipping the card inside her purse, she got into her car and drove away. She traveled down Broadway, heading south to her apartment on 2nd Avenue, near Pike Place. The busy Seattle boulevard was crowded this time of night.

Finally, Lillian arrived at her home, hurried into the big apartment complex, and rode the elevator to the seventh floor. After walking down the small hallway to her apartment, she unlocked the deadbolt and pushed the heavy door open. When she stepped inside, she was ceremoniously greeted by her house cat, Rebel, who appeared at her feet, purring eagerly, wanting to be fed.

Turning around, Lillian glanced down the hall to see if anyone was there. Seeing nothing unusual, she closed her door, locked the deadbolt, and placed a small security chain on the doorjamb.

Her friend Amy had insisted this male friend of hers was the perfect match—even going as far as to say that he could be "the one." Nonetheless, a nagging nervousness like she had never felt clouded her emotions.

Reaching inside the cupboard for Rebel's favorite cat food, she pulled hard on the aluminum tab, plopped the smelly fish mush into the small dish, and then put it on the floor. She hurriedly jumped into the shower. Afterward, feeling hungry, she thought this diet would be her death and grabbed some low-carb melba toast to ease her hunger. Returning to her bedroom, she rummaged through her closet.

Although it had been days since she started this new diet, every size ten dress she tried on fit painfully tight. It was time for the old standby, the size twelve black dress that always seemed to work in a pinch. After putting it on she looked at her reflection in the mirror and considered herself dashing.

After brushing her blonde hair, she was ready to meet her date. She applied her makeup with a quick hand and slipped on her high heels. The finishing touch was a final spray of that expensive cologne she had gotten for Christmas. Looking over at Rebel, she made a pose and announced, "Tell me, what do you think?"

Rebel, too busy eating, ignored her comment as he devoured his last remnants of mush. Lillian tenderly looked down and ordered him to behave himself.

Grabbing her purse and coat from the closet, Lillian left her apartment and locked the door behind her. Feeling like she was late, she rushed to the elevator, pushed the button, and waited.

A squeaky apartment door opened behind her, and she saw a woman struggling to get out of her apartment with a baby-filled stroller and diaper bag in her arm. Was her neighbor Kathy finally free from the doorway?

Kathy looked up to see Lillian waiting for the elevator and pleasantly greeted her with a smile.

Holding onto the stroller's handle, Kathy stood erect, readjusted her load to one shoulder, and walked to the elevator. "Someone looks like they have a hot date," she replied with a grin.

"A blind date my friend has set me up with," Lillian replied, unexcited.

Kathy laughed and said, "You know those rarely work out."

"I know, but I have to try," she said. "If not, just to get my mother off my back!"

"Yes, I understand what you're going through. I, too, have a mother who would constantly bug me about finding Mr. Right!" Kathy laughed.

"I know. Is that all we are to our mothers, baby machines?"

"Have you ever gotten phone calls reminding you that you're getting older and that your dear mother wants a grandchild before she's too old to play with them?"

"Constantly! Once, I told my mother I had lost my phone, so I wouldn't have to talk to her and be bugged about having kids. To make matters worse, she started calling me at work!"

Looking down at the three-month-old child, Lillian commented, "Look how beautiful Amber is becoming."

"Thank you," Kathy replied. "You know she gets that from my side of the family."

Looking up at Kathy, Lillian said, "Well, of course, she does. I've seen Andy in the daylight."

Both women broke out in contagious laughter.

The elevator arrived, and the door slowly opened. The women rode it down to the lobby and walked outside to the sidewalk.

Kathy looked back at her and said, "I hope everything works out for you this evening, and he's the one!"

"Thank you, Kathy. I do, too. I have to run. I'll see you soon and share how the evening went."

"Okay, that's a promise. Take care of yourself," she said.

The women parted ways.

Lillian had only taken a few steps when she stopped and turned to Kathy, calling her back.

"Yes—what is it? Did I drop Amber's pacifier again?"

"No, Kathy, before you go—can I get your opinion on something?"

"Sure, what is it?"

Reaching into her purse, Lillian pulled out the small card she received on her windshield and handed it to her. "I found this on my car earlier. Could you read it and tell me what you think?"

"Sure, hand it over."

A minute later, the expression on Kathy's face was puzzled. She handed it back to Lillian, "I don't know. It seems very strange to me."

"Yeah, I would agree."

"What do you plan to do?"

"Not much. What can I do? I keep thinking someone at work is playing a game on me."

"A sick game, if you ask me!"

"Well, I wanted your opinion, and you gave it. Thank you, Kathy. As I said, I'm not sure what it means. But I don't have time to worry about it now. I'll talk to you later. I have to run."

Lillian arrived at her car, parked in the apartment parking lot, and sped to the restaurant. She was running late, and yes, there is that "making a grand entrance" thing that some do on purpose as a way to impress. But this wasn't that. If he were any gentleman, he would certainly understand her being late to their date.

As she drove, other thoughts invaded her thinking, and she remembered blind dates from the past that weren't the best. Sometimes after meeting for the first time, she wouldn't be to their liking, or they weren't to her liking. There had to be an attraction between both parties.

Throughout any dating experience, she'd realized there must be that spark; without that burning desire for each other's existence, one would never give themselves freely to what you could call love.

She thought she'd been ready to commit a few times in the past, but the relationship would ultimately prove dull after a short time. Afterward, she was nothing more than a plaything to a boyfriend who expected her to stay home alone and wait for his triumphant entry with wanton breath, unable to survive without his attention. *Oh, brother,* she smirked.

No, that's not me, she thought. *I am a capable woman who needs to stop searching for Mr. Right and be content with my life. Just me and Rebel. If only Mother would understand this and let nature take its course!*

Without warning, the car in front slammed on its brakes, causing her to skid and swerve into the other lane to avoid a collision.

Damn it, that was close, she thought. Why was she still living in the heart of the city? This living on top of each other was sometimes annoying, and she remembered it wasn't like this growing up back in the Midwest out on the plains.

Four years ago, she moved to Seattle after college and got a job working in a local newspaper as a digital specialist sales representative. She enjoyed being on her own for the first time, but she discovered the competition in this line of work was fierce and soon realized it was a dog-eat-dog world.

Driving in the traffic was tough this time of night, especially on a Friday evening, and the rain hampered her visibility to see the cars weaving in and out of traffic. Driving in these conditions was quickly becoming a pain. Still, she arrived at the restaurant ten minutes late, promptly parked her car on the street, and casually walked inside the busy place to look for the man she was to meet.

Lillian saw a waving hand at the booth near the back. While she approached the stranger, what she saw so far impressed her: a tall, bleached blond man with a muscular build who stood up.

"Hello, you must be Lillian," he said.

"Yes! Hello, how are you?" she replied with a pleasant smile.

"Amy has told me so much about you; I couldn't wait

to meet you. My name is Andrew Jenkins. Truthfully, these blind dates are so awkward, and you never know what the other person will turn up at all. But I must say I like what I see! I hope you don't mind. I already had a drink while waiting."

"Not at all. I agree that dating is awkward—thank you for the compliment," Lillian replied graciously.

"No, thank you for showing up. I'm more nervous than ever. I hope you don't mind, but I need another drink."

Looking toward the kitchen, Andrew whistled for the waitress to come over. While they waited, Andrew suggested they have a seat.

"Yes, noble idea."

Getting comfortable, he asked, "Um, would you like something to drink? Most chicks like white wine—right? Sure, they do—it makes their blood hot."

"No, thank you. I'm not the typical 'chick,' as you put it. Water will suffice. After all, I don't know you, and getting sozzled wouldn't be proper."

"Boy, you sure are pretty."

"Yes, you already said that," Lillian replied, embarrassed by the attention.

"Sure, I knew that. But boy, ain't I the lucky one."

"Lucky?" She wasn't sure what he meant.

The waitress came to the booth and introduced herself as Amanda. While handing them a menu, she pleasantly asked for their drink orders.

Andrew spoke up. "I'll take another double scotch. This time give me a little boost, will you please? That last drink tasted a little watered down!"

"Yes, of course. I'll have a word with the bartender."

Then, turning to Lillian, Amanda asked, "Miss, what can I get you this evening?"

Before Lillian could say anything, Andrew shouted,

"She'll be having water—no hot-blooded woman tonight, I can tell you."

Ignoring his comment, Lillian said, "Yes, water, thank you," feeling a little embarrassed by her date.

After the waitress disappeared, Andrew quickly apologized. "I shouldn't talk like that. I'm sorry. Sometimes I can say the stupidest things." He downed the rest of his scotch.

"That's okay, Andrew. Let's put it behind us, all right?"

"Sure, that sounds great."

"So, Andrew, what do you do for a living?" Lillian asked.

"Well, I'm not a millionaire if that's what you want to know," he responded callously.

"No, of course not. I'm just making conversation," Lillian said, feeling cautious with her next question.

"Well, I work hard at selling vacuums for a local department store. It's not what I want to do for the rest of my life, but for now, it pays the bills," he said. "I heard from Amy that you're an investment broker or something like that."

"I work as a secretary for a brokerage house; I'm not an authentic investment broker yet," she explained.

"Yay, okay, I get it," Andrew said rudely.

"Oh, all right, never mind then," Lillian replied, becoming irritated by this guy's behavior.

The waitress appeared with their drinks and pleasantly asked what they would like to have for dinner.

"Well, I'll take a beef filet and a baked potato covered with sour cream sprinkled with chives and bacon bits," Andrew ordered, then added, "Put a rush on that, will you? I'm hungry. My date was a little late getting here."

The waitress asked Lillian, "What will you have,

ma'am?"

"I'll have a chicken salad with a vinaigrette dressing, please."

"Okay, got it. Thank you." She wrote everything down on her order pad and walked away.

"It figures. I knew for sure you would order rabbit food," Andrew yelled. "Give me a good old steak any day; I never could stand to eat that green stuff. Nope, just couldn't acquire a taste for lettuce." Looking around, he announced, "Shit, I'm hungry. Hopefully, dinner won't be too long. I knew I should have stopped and got a cheap burger before I came." Afterward, he took a long drink from his glass, emptying the entire contents in one gulp.

"I choose to eat healthily," Lillian said. "Besides, I'm always a little nervous on these blind dates."

"Oh, I know all about you, chicks, believe me. Do you mind if I ask you a personal question?" Andrew said boldly.

"Sure, that would be all right."

"Could you tell me what color panties you are wearing tonight?" Andrew asked with a smile.

"What! What does that have to do with anything?" Lillian asked, feeling uncomfortable with his stupid question.

"It's simple—if you're wearing black or red panties, then I'm getting lucky tonight."

"Excuse me? I'm not telling you the color of my underwear; I'm not that type of girl. Besides, Amy said you were a gentleman. But you're certainly not acting like one, let me tell you!"

"Oh, I get it. You're the same as the other girls Amy has tried to hook me up with."

"Tell me, Amy tried to hook you up with other girls?" Lillian asked now, demanding an answer for why she found herself in this situation.

"Oh, you know, being a friend of the family and all, she was doing you a favor. She explained that you were having difficulty meeting that special guy, and you were becoming desperate before your maternity clock expired, so she wanted to help you out," he boasted through slurred words.

"Amy, huh! Desperately needing someone? Okay, I'm beginning to understand what's happening here." Abruptly, Lillian said, "Will you please excuse me?"

"Sure thing, sweets. Go ahead and take a pee break if you have to," Andrew remarked, looking around for the waitress so he could order another drink.

"Thank you, um, I think?" she remarked, standing.

Leaving the table, knowing that this night was over, she walked to the back of the restaurant to the ladies restroom. On her way there, she ran into the waitress who had taken their order only a moment ago.

"Hello, Amanda, is it?" Lillian asked.

"Yes, can I help?" she said.

"You sure can. This blind date was not at all what I expected. Could you please be so kind as to cancel my order? I choose not to stay."

"Sure, I completely understand. No Prince Charming, huh?" Amanda answered.

"Oh, no, not even a frog prince but a mistake from a soon-to-be ex-girlfriend! I knew it was over when the guy asked me about the color of my panties—right! After that, I felt it was time to leave," Lillian announced.

"Oh, I agree." Then, looking back toward where Andrew was seated, Amanda added, "What a creep!"

"I had no way of knowing just how creepy he was until a short time ago. Is there another way out of here? I don't want to be seen leaving your restaurant."

"Yes, of course. Let's go through the kitchen. Follow me. I'll show you the way out."

Lillian followed the waitress through the hot kitchen, walking past the hot stoves and steel sinks filled with metal pans piled high, and soon arrived at a back door.

Amanda opened it to the outside, turned, and said, "Walk around the side of the building, and you'll come upon a chain-link gate. Unlatch it and go through it. On the other end of the fence, you will see the street."

"Thank you so much. I could never repay you for your kindness," Lillian replied, grateful to be free of the situation.

"Look, we girls have to stay together," Amanda replied. "Now go. I have to get back to work. Be safe, okay?"

"I will," Lillian replied and disappeared into the darkness.

When Lillian arrived back at her car, she was grateful to make her exit, clean and unnoticed. After starting her vehicle, the windshield wipers and defroster made it possible to see well enough to drive. Unfortunately, she had to pass the restaurant's front entrance as she left the area. As she did, she glanced at the front door, and there stood Andrew arguing with Amanda, the waitress, and the manager. *Probably about the fact that he's now dining alone.*

On her way back home, her anger grew hot as she thought of Amy telling this man that she was desperate and in need of someone in her life. *The fact is that I'm happy to be just single.* After earning her business degree and living on her own, supporting herself all this time, her life was complete. She didn't have to complicate things by introducing a new man into her life.

On the way home, she continued her angry retort by

yelling in the car, "I'm not desperate, as Amy so happily broadcasted to this Andrew character!"

When she arrived home, she found twelve messages on her answering machine—all undoubtedly from this Andrew wanting to know what happened to her and why she left the restaurant. Truthfully, as soon as she walked into her apartment and locked the door behind her, all she could think of was slipping out of this dress and changing into something more comfortable, perhaps her favorite pair of sweats.

She then ate something light, opened a bottle of her favorite wine, snuggled up on her couch, and began reading a book.

The truth was that she was pretty hungry and would have stayed at the restaurant if her date from hell hadn't become so rude. After all, he wasn't bad-looking but lacked good manners around a lady.

As she sat on the couch sipping on her glass of Pinot, she remembered the extraordinarily unpretentious card left on her car windshield. Wanting to read it once more, she got up, went into her bedroom, found her purse, took out the little gold card, and began reading it.

Who on earth would be following me? After reading it a second time, she set it on her dresser, then returned to the couch and her favorite book.

Feeling tired and ready for bed, she set her book down and shut off the lights. Surprisingly, her cell phone rang. When she retrieved it from her purse, she saw Amy's number.

It was late, and she was undecided whether to engage in this matter about Andrew now or do it in the morning, although she still felt angry about the situation. She surprised herself when she flicked the phone open and said, "Yes, can I help you, Amy?"

"Why did you leave my friend back at the restaurant?" Amy shouted.

"Speaking of your friend Andrew, let me ask you a question, Amy. Did you tell him that I was desperate and needed someone in my life?"

"Well, no, not really. I might have said that you hadn't dated in a while. You even said you're tired of meeting all the wrong guys and wanted to meet someone nice for a change."

"Some good man—really!" Lillian answered. "That lovely friend of yours was half drunk when I arrived at the restaurant, and it went downhill fast."

"Well, I have Andrew here with me, and he feels terrible that you left so hurriedly," Amy said.

"Listen, when a guy asks me what color panties I'm wearing, meaning that I'm ready for lovemaking, the date is over, as far as I'm concerned," Lillian retorted.

"Oh, he didn't mean anything by it—it's just Andrew's way of being funny and breaking the ice. He is a good man and has always acted like a gentleman around my family. He feels his behavior was atrocious and wants to come to your apartment and explain things better; he even promises to behave himself. All he asks is for a chance to explain; he won't be at your place long."

"No, not tonight. I'm not in the mood for company," Lillian replied.

"Oh, come on. I'll give him your address so he can drop by and apologize."

"Oh no, you don't," Lillian protested but heard the call ended abruptly.

Damn it, Amy. I don't want to deal with this guy at this time of night. She looked over at the bat she kept by the front door, but it gave her little comfort. Andrew was over six feet tall. He could hold his own. Still, she decided she would not even open the front door if he showed up.

She redialed Amy's number and heard nothing but the ringing tone. She knew Amy wouldn't answer the phone, which made Lillian even angrier about this situation and the soon-to-arrive unwelcomed guest.

Within a half hour, she heard knocking on her front door. At first, she thought she might ignore the knocking, hoping he would go away. But her parents taught her to confront her fears, not disregard her problem,s but to face them head-on, which is what she planned on doing with this Andrew.

"It's me, Andrew. Please open the door."

With a long sigh, she walked over to the closed door and shouted loud enough so he couldn't mistake her wishes. "Andrew, please leave. I don't want to engage in any conversation at this hour. It's late. I want you to go."

"I'm not leaving until you agree to have dinner with me," Andrew shouted through the door.

"That's not a good idea," Lillian replied. "Please listen, I want you to leave. I don't wish to be rude, or else you will force me to call the police."

"Go ahead and call them; I don't care. Many of my friends are on the force, and they won't do a damn thing. Come on, just agree to have dinner once more, and I promise I will never harass you again," Andrew said.

"No. What part of no don't you understand?" Lillian demanded, with no compromising in her determination.

"If you continue to say no, I will stay here all night and bang on your door until you open it and talk to me. Remember the wolf—I'll huff and puff and blow your door down."

Having nosy neighbors can be a benefit and a blessing. In her apartment building, this was the case with Mrs. Hockings, who, upon hearing the commotion outside in the hallway, immediately called the police.

Lillian paced back and forth for several minutes, hearing the constant pounding, until she heard other voices talking outside her front door. Then she heard a different type of knocking and the voices of other men who identified themselves as Officers Hargrove and Bennet.

Looking through the peephole, she saw the shining badge and blue uniform on the other end. Quickly unlatching the chain and the deadbolt, she opened the door and saw Andrew detained by one officer while the other looked at her.

"Hello, ma'am, my name is Officer Hargrove. Is this gentleman disturbing you?"

"I asked him to leave, but he wouldn't," Lillian replied.

"Lillian, it's me," Andrew shouted, wanting to escape the officer's grip.

"Yes, Andrew, I asked you to leave, but you wouldn't. Now, look what happened," Lillian responded.

"It's evident this man has had too much to drink this evening. We plan on taking him downtown and arresting him for public intoxication," Hargrove said.

"Hey, what do we have here?" Officer Bennet announced, holding a large pocketknife that he had removed from inside Andrew's coat.

"Hey, I can carry that. It's perfectly legal," Andrew argued.

"Sure, it is," Officer Hargrove replied, smiling. "But tonight, it isn't. You're going downtown with us."

Turning to Lillian, Hargrove took out a small pad of paper and said, "Could I get your name and some information for our records?"

"Certainly, Officer, whatever you need. My full name is Lillian Newburg."

"Ma'am, is this your correct address?" he asked while writing in his notepad.

"Yes," she answered softly.

Click. Andrew was handcuffed with his hands behind his back. Instantly, he stared back at Lillian with an ugly scowl that wasn't flattering to his good looks.

The police radio suddenly blurted out a call for Hargrove to respond. "Go ahead, dispatch. Hargrove here."

"We received a report of a disturbance a block away from your location. Can you respond?" the voice on the radio said.

"Yes, on our way, dispatch."

Turning to Lillian, Officer Hargrove said, "Well, ma'am, we have all we need. Here's my business card. Please call the station if you require further assistance."

He then tipped his hat and turned to his partner. "Let's go."

Lillian watched as they escorted Andrew from her building. Somehow she felt relieved that he was going; maybe all of this was just a misunderstanding—or perhaps it wasn't—but the mere fact that he was carrying a knife left her feeling vulnerable and scared. Glancing over at Mrs. Hockings, she thanked her for calling the police.

Mrs. Hockings, whose cat was busy purring at her feet, said, "You can't be too careful these days." Then she reached down, picked up the animal, and disappeared inside her apartment, closing the door with a thud.

Hearing the locking mechanism turn on the door's other side, Lillian knew she was safe again, back in her private world.

With enough excitement for one day, Lillian felt exhausted and returned to her apartment. She knew there would be no sleep tonight. The possible realization that perhaps Andrew was a serial killer or rapist made her shudder with a new fear of how close she could have come to death.

The blinking of the answering machine indicated a message, but she did not care who had left it. She was in no mood to listen to any message. Instead, she walked over and unplugged the machine from the wall. Hopefully, no other troubles would occur for the rest of the night. She flicked on the television to her favorite romance channel.

On her coffee table was her glass of wine that she hadn't finished—no doubt tonight would be the best reason to empty the bottle. But, instead, she took a sip and set down her glass.

She gasped in fright as she saw an image of someone dressed all in black standing behind her in the reflection of her living room mirror. A set of hands grabbed her around her neck. The intruder's grip tightened. She tried to scream for help, but no words came out.

Her world and all she had known, her struggles to achieve a future for herself, no longer mattered—an approaching blackness clouded her vision as the hands wrapped around her throat tightened, cutting off the air to her lungs. Struggling against the forces ending her life, she reached behind and slapped the intruder's face, kicking and screaming out in desperation for someone to hear her. She prayed that someone would overhear her struggling inside her apartment building. Sadly, her cries failed her.

Yet, she continued to struggle, knowing all would be lost if she surrendered. As a result, she jerked her head from side to side and, in a desperate attempt, grabbed ahold of the person's arms. Despite her pulling at her intruder's arms as hard as she could, the strength of this individual surpassed her own.

Tears of regret began flowing down her cheeks. No longer would she see a future with a loving family filled with children's laughter. No, her world grew dark all around her. In a last desperate attempt, she again reached up and slapped at the face behind the mask. But the hands around her throat tightened even more.

Unable to resist, she took her last breath, surrendering to the forces of her demise.

Chapter 2

"Well, from what I can see, the murderer came through the open patio door," Detective Max Mulholland announced to his partner, Ben Holder. "I found unusual footprints across the floor. What is uncertain is how could somebody crawl up seven stories on this side of the apartment building and not be seen?"

"I see the victim has a cat. No doubt she kept the sliding door open to allow her cat to come and go freely," Holder remarked.

"Have you noticed the cat hasn't left her side this entire time we've been here?"

Taking his pen, Mulholland moved Lillian's hair from her face. Her expression was one of sadness.

"I see she was strangled," said Mulholland. "Hopefully, we don't have a serial killer on our hands."

"It doesn't appear to be. No other reports in the area of another murder matching this description."

"Did you take note of the underpants stuck in her mouth?"

"I suppose it belongs to the victim. Once the lab guys examine the body, we'll know for sure."

"So, talking about the body, what do you think? She's been dead for what? Forty hours, at least?" Mulholland asked.

"That would be my estimation. I don't see any sign of sexual assault—the victim still wears all her clothing—but we can't be sure until the crime lab shows up."

"According to what I've learned thus far, she was reported missing by a coworker named Amy. Earlier, we were called to this scene for a disturbance involving a drunk boyfriend named Andrew."

"Well, it seems to me it's an open-and-shut case; it's quite obvious he's our killer?" Holder remarked.

"No, not so fast. The boyfriend was arrested that night and has spent the last two days locked behind bars waiting to be bailed out, so he couldn't have done it."

A group of investigators from the coroner's office entered the room, set down their tote boxes, and began examining the crime scene and the body. They tested her liver with a temperature probe and determined she had been dead for approximately forty-eight hours, as Mulholland had guessed. As suspected, there was no sign of sexual assault.

They searched the entire apartment for clues, took pictures, and dusted for fingerprints. When Barclay, the lead investigator, removed the panties, he noticed blood inside the crotch of the fabric.

"What do we have here?" said Barclay.

"Did you find something?" Max asked.

"I'll have to run a blood analysis to determine if the blood belongs to the killer or the victim. I'll let you know more when the coroner does an autopsy."

According to the trained police detectives, the murderer undoubtedly found satisfaction from strangulation as their way of experiencing domination over the victim. They would feel the life leaving the person's body. No doubt they were dealing with a loner, someone who couldn't adjust to society, or someone with a problem with the ladies and couldn't get it up.

As the detectives discussed the details further, the CSI

investigator handed Mulholland a small envelope they found stuffed inside Lillian's purse.

"What's this?" Mulholland asked.

"I'm not sure, but I found it inside the victim's purse. Read it; I believe you'll find it quite interesting," Barclay reported.

"I already looked inside her purse. All I found was her wallet but nothing particular inside. You say you found this envelope inside her purse, uh?"

"You see, that's what I've been saying all along. You need glasses, Max! Best accept it, man. Now it's affecting your job as an investigator."

"Bullshit, Ben. Now you're sounding like my wife!"

"Whatever you say! Now open the damn envelope."

"Wait—Barclay, did you brush this for prints?"

"Yes, certainly. We found two sets of prints, one we believe is the victim's prints, and the other we'll have to check to see if they're in our database."

"That's strange, Ben. Listen to this: It's addressed to 'Dear Someone.' Already it sounds kooky to me!"

Max opened the letter and read the contents aloud.

Dear Someone,

I realize you don't know me. You probably think this strange. Regardless of your opinions, the outcome will be the same. These violent delights have violent ends.

Signed,
Concerned

"What the hell does that mean?" Ben asked.

Barclay announced, "It's a quote from Shakespeare's *Romeo and Juliet*, spoken by Friar Lawrence in a conversation with Romeo in Act 2, Scene 6. Didn't you guys study literature in high school?"

Max thought for a few moments before answering. Examining the card closer, he concluded that either the killer wrote the note to announce his intent to kill Lillian, or someone else had seen the killer stalking his victim and wanted to warn her.

"Ben, I'm afraid we have a disturbing trend. Hopefully, we don't run across any more of these warning cards. If we do, it may mean we have a new breed of killer, one able to climb high buildings—perhaps a circus freak or someone like that!"

"Hey, Max, wasn't there a full moon last night? When that usually happens, the freaks come out of the shadows, wanting to play. Another thing, wasn't the circus in town recently?"

"Oh, that was a couple of weeks ago, nothing recently. Either way, if there was a witness who saw Lillian's murderer, we need to find that person immediately."

A commotion at the door turned out to be two guys working for the morgue to collect Lillian's body. With approval from the crime lab, the men dressed in white carried a stretcher inside the room and set it next to the young girl's body. Next, they unfurled a black plastic bag, unzipped it down its entire length, and pulled it open. Shooing the cat aside, they took Lillian's body by her ankles and arms. They lifted her body and set her down inside the bag, zipped it up, placed it on the gurney, and rolled her body out the door.

As they left the room, the cat watched his master being carried away, no longer to return. It sat there, not moving for some time, as the two detectives continued their investigation.

A fact none would contest was that Lillian's body, in its state of decomposition, filled the room with a foul odor. Ben hurried to open all the windows in the small apartment.

A crowd gathered outside in the hallway, watching the young woman's remains carried away on a stretcher. Having gathered all the evidence, they could—no fingerprints or other suitable evidence were recovered—the two detectives turned to leave.

For now, having given orders to the uniformed officers to secure the crime scene, the apartment would be protected with caution tape and the door locked.

Max, an avid cat lover, stared down at the abandoned cat. Somehow the cat knew they were about to leave, and, as a judge of good character, he hurried over, wrapped himself around Max's feet, and began purring.

Ben laughed aloud, seeing his partner's situation, and said, "Looks like someone needs a new home."

Shoving his notebook in his coat pocket, Max reached down, picked up the cat in his arms, and began rubbing his chin.

"Are you all alone now?" said Max. "Your mommy is not returning, is she? I'll tell you what, I live alone. You can come live with me if you want. What do you say?"

Not surprisingly, the cat began to purr.

"Come on, let's get out of here. I'll contact your owner's family to see if anyone wants you. If not, you got a place with me, pal!"

Turning to his partner, Max said, "Ben, be a pal, will you? Gather the cat's food and water bowls and any food you find. It's important not to mix their food, especially if they have a special diet."

"A special diet, Max? Sometimes I don't know about you, old buddy."

"Sure, whatever you say. Listen, I'll collect the cat's litter tray."

Sometime later, when they appeared in the hallway, they were met by an elderly neighbor shaken by the news of the young girl's demise, who approached the detectives and said, "I just knew something would happen to that poor girl! It's not safe living in the big city by yourself anymore."

Max asked, "Excuse me, ma'am, what did you say your name was?"

"I'm Lillian's neighbor Mrs. Hockings. I was the one who called the police the other night when that cad came to her door and demanded that she come outside to talk to him. I could tell the man was drunk and feared for the young girl's safety, you understand."

"Listen, Mrs. Hockings, can you tell me if you heard anything strange in Lillian's apartment later that night?"

"No, no strange noises or nothing like that. You must understand I usually go to bed early. The other night I only heard that commotion when that nasty man came over to Lillian's apartment demanding to be let inside. Oh my, I was so frightened and thought he would burst through the door. Then I'd have to come over and beat him with my purse! Gratefully, the police arrived in the nick of time to arrest him. Tell me, Detectives, do you believe that man killed poor Lillian?"

"We cannot say, you understand. Too early in our investigation."

"Oh, I see."

Handing the cat to a rookie officer, Max gave a business card to the woman and said, "Listen, Mrs. Hockings, if you can think of anything you might have forgotten, my partner and I are always available. Just call the number on the card. Sometimes some things don't seem important now but will come back to you later."

"What do you plan to do with Lillian's cat?"

"Oh, we'll contact the family to see if anyone wants him. For now, please don't forget to call us if you remember anything. Good evening. We must be off."

The two detectives turned to leave, ignoring the crowd of people lingering in the hallway who was watching them and whispering to one another.

When they reached the elevators, the cat seemed troubled and hissed while digging his claws into Max's forearms, his hair standing on end. Max turned to see the distressed cat, then saw the shadow of someone turning the corner.

"Shit—Max, what did you do to the cat?" Ben joked.

"Nothing. I haven't done anything."

Max turned back to look at the vacant hallway. The seasoned detective had an eerie feeling. *Perhaps the cat saw his owner's killer? Maybe they're close by, in the crowd of people, watching and waiting for another chance to murder.*

Turning back around, Max said, "We have to catch this guy. I fear there will soon be more bodies if we don't."

"We'll do our best. You know that."

"Yes, our best. Is it good enough, or will we be too late, much like the Stonehenge case?"

"The Stonehenge case, no—not another case like that! I hope you're wrong, buddy."

"Me, too. Let's get out of here!"

When the detectives arrived downstairs and got into their vehicle, Max turned to Ben and said, "Hey, you didn't happen to see an animal carrier by chance in the girl's apartment, did you?"

"Shit, man, I don't know. Look, Max, why this fetish for cats? Come on, we have a murder case on our hands, and all you're worried about is this stupid cat!"

"No, listen to me. You don't get it. It would make transporting the animal easier for us. Besides, my arm is bleeding. That cat saw something or someone. It reacted naturally by hissing at the menace. I'm sure this cat saw the murderer!"

"Are we ever going to get out of here? Fine, you stay here, and I'll go back up to the apartment and see if I can find a cat carrier for your friend."

"Thank you, Ben."

Now with one thing on his mind, Ben hurried back up to Lillian's apartment. When he rode the elevator to the seventh floor, he passed two uniformed officers leaving.

"Officer, did you secure the crime scene?"

"Yes, per protocol."

"Look, my partner downstairs wants me to search the apartment to see if there's a carrier for the cat. Could you let me back inside?"

"Sure, no problem."

Turning to the other officer, he told him to go ahead and leave, and he'd meet him at the squad car.

When they arrived, the police officer took out a set of keys belonging to the deceased and pulled the caution tape off the exterior door. Unlocking the door, Ben walked in.

The apartment was completely dark. The only light was what filtered in from the outside neon lights of the city. The smell of death was thick in the air. Curtains swayed side to side as the passing breeze pulled them open. He felt an eerie stillness in the space. The shadows and sounds of the city echoed outside.

Determined to return to the station, Ben ignored the creepy place and walked back to the bedroom.

He approached the bedroom nightstand to switch on the small lamp. He walked to the closet in the soft glow, pulled the doors apart, and looked upon the top shelf. Seeing no cat carrier, he closed the doors again and turned around. Although he couldn't be sure, he felt he was being watched.

Was it the recently dead eyeing him or his activities getting the better of him? Not a man who so quickly fell to superstitions, he'd seen enough death in his career to warrant a thick-skin attitude. But here, menacing darkness lingered, hidden in the shadows. With nothing else to see, he returned to the lamp and switched it off.

He walked into the kitchen, avoiding the stained carpet where the young girl met her end. He envisioned her body lying there, all alone.

Ben reached for his service revolver. Somehow it felt comforting to know it was close, strapped to his hip.

Turning on the kitchen lights, Ben approached the small pantry, opened the door, and looked inside. There at the bottom, on the floor, was the cat carrier.

He grabbed the plastic crate and closed the pantry door. When he reached the front door hallway, he lifted the yellow caution tape and walked out.

"I see you got what you wanted?" the officer asked.

"Yeah, the carrier."

"Are you ready to leave?"

Lost in contemplation, Ben stared into the darkness of the apartment as if he was expecting something to move within the shadows.

"What? Yes, close it up."

The officer closed the door and locked it tightly, placing the caution tape back into place. The two left, and when they walked down the hallway, the nosy neighbors eyeing them, closed their doors, and they heard the sound of chains being set into place.

When Ben appeared downstairs, he saw Max sitting in the car, holding the cat in his arms. Ben opened the car door.

"Here is your damn cat carrier," Ben said.

"Great, the cat and I appreciate your efforts. Are you

ready? I got a call from the captain. He wants to see us back at the station."

"Yeah, give me a minute."

Closing the car door, Ben walked over to the side of the building and looked up toward the seventh floor. The ominous building stood erect, uncaring. The fire escape metal railing mounted to the outside was the logical choice to enter the girl's apartment. As Ben stood there looking up into the gray clouds overhead, he searched the shadows for any sign. Back in the apartment, his hair stood on end, as if someone was there in that place with him. Perhaps the lone killer still lurked there, enjoying his handiwork.

Unexpectedly, a distant car horn blasted around the corner.

Turning to leave, Ben walked a few steps and stopped, taking another look up. High in the shadows, he thought he saw movement in the corner of the building. He froze in place, concentrating on the structure. He was disturbed by yet another salvo from the car's blasting horns.

Ben slowly and deliberately walked away. In his heart, he felt something or someone was there hiding. For now, he had to get going.

The murderer—was this his first victim? Or was there a long line of murders still yet to be discovered? The killer, unafraid of heights, had used this talent to their advantage. Still, why the note in the girl's purse? Why the underwear in the victim's mouth? Were these two facts linked, or were they separate events in the making?

The fire escape—look again at the fire escape, he told himself. *Time to leave.* Then he took a final glance up at the clouds.

Seeing nothing, the detective left the crime scene, the place where Lillian met her end. A life once so promising was now alone at the morgue, cold and sitting on a slab.

Chapter 3

On a sunny day, two young women were leaving the playhouse where they performed two shows a night as backup performers in Shakespeare's *Macbeth*. They walked down the busy sidewalk and approached their parked car. Unlocking it, the two crawled inside and started to pull away from the curb.

"Peggy, stop the car for a minute!" Marsha yelled out. "There's something stuck to the windshield."

Hopping out of the passenger side, Marsha reached around to remove a small envelope under the windshield wipers. After retrieving the card, she jumped back inside. Peggy's car sped down the busy boulevard, back to a meeting with their friends.

Seeing her friend holding something in her hands, Peggy asked, "What's that?"

"I don't know. It's a small card of some sort. It's addressed to 'Dear Someone.' Sounds weird."

"Go ahead and open it. Let's see what it says—you know it might be from David, the choreographer assistant who can't keep his eyes off you. Perhaps he's expressing his devoted love and wants to go out or something."

"Peggy, you do realize he's gay, right?"

"Nonsense. That's just a rumor made up by his ex-girlfriend who got dumped on her birthday—I don't believe it! Go on, hurry. I want to know what it says."

"Okay, whatever. I'll open the stupid card. Just give

me a minute."

"Sure, take your time. I want to know—shit, hang on."

Peggy hit her brakes to avoid smashing into the rear end of another car. The small compact vehicle screeched to a stop.

"Peggy, would you please watch the damn road and pay attention to where you're going?"

"Yes, yes, hurry and open the card."

"All right, here it is."

Dear Someone,
You probably think this strange. I realize you don't know me.
Regardless of your opinions, the outcome will be the same. There's beggary in the love that can be reckoned.
Signed,
The Witness

"I know that line! It's from *Antony and Cleopatra*, Act 1, Scene 1, Line 15. I was once backup for the leading role. What in the hell does that mean to us: 'There's beggary in the love that can be reckoned?'" Peggy asked.

"I don't know. Geez, I thought for sure it was a dinner invitation or something. Now I'm not so sure. Hey, whom do you suppose the card was meant for?"

"What do you mean?"

"Well, it's your car, right? The obvious choice would be that the card was meant for you! But we are always together, roommates and all. The fact that I don't own a car and I'm always hitching a ride with you could mean the card was supposed to be for me—oh, I'm not sure. I thought the card was placed nearer the passenger side of the car. If the card was meant for me, what does that mean? Wow—man, that's freaky!"

Marsha, still holding the card in her hand, seemed troubled. Peggy looked over, ignoring Marsha's response, and hurriedly drove downtown to the bar where they met their friends. When they parked on the busy streets and hurried inside, after spotting their friends sitting outside on the patio, they walked past a small gate and joined them outside.

The cast members were arguing about tonight's performance in a heated conversation. Everyone at the table sounded off about what the choreographer had done to their roles in the play.

Just as Peggy pulled out a chair to sit down, André asked, "Did you hear what Marshall has done to your part in the play? Why, he's cut out your piece—completely!"

"What, no—damn it, I felt something was up when he asked me how fond I was of being a singing witch at practice. It was the only part in the play where I could broadcast my talents."

"Oh, who knows? Maybe there is something special he's planning."

Marsha listened, saying nothing, still troubled by the card in her hand.

When the conversation changed and was directed toward her, Susan announced, "Too bad we didn't have your part!"

"My part, what? The musical score for the orchestra?"

"Yeah, I would agree," Marianne said. "At least we wouldn't be facing the possibility of being laid off."

"Yes, I suppose," Marsha responded.

She was lost in thought, troubled.

André, more perceptive than most, announced, "Marsha, tell us, what has you so bugged, girlfriend?"

"What?"

Turning to the group, André announced, "Hey, listen for a second, will you all? Tell us, please. Something is troubling our friend. Will you please tell us what it is?"

"Tell you what?"

"Go on. Tell them about the card," Peggy suggested.

"Oh, this card?" Marsha said, holding the small item in her hand.

The waitress appeared, deposited menus on the table, and asked, "Hello, will you have anything to drink?"

"Boy, would I," Peggy screamed.

"Give me a glass of Chardonnay," Marsha announced.

"I'll take a Malbec."

"Fine, okay, would any of you like to order anything from the menu?" the waitress asked.

"Sure—yes, give me a club sandwich," Peggy announced.

"I'll take a cheeseburger, no onions or pickles!"

"Fine. I'll return shortly with your drinks."

"Thank you," Peggy replied and handed back the menus.

After the waitress left, Marianne turned to Marsha and said, "All right, now tell us about this card!"

"It's the strangest thing. When we got to Peggy's car, this card was stuck under the wipers."

"What does it say?" André asked.

"Oh, here. You read it," Marsha announced and handed over the card.

When André read the card aloud, the group stared at each other in disbelief.

"The first part almost seems like a warning of some type," André said. "That's freaking weird. 'Regardless of your opinions, the outcome will be the same. There's beggary in the love that can be reckoned.' I recognize the line from *Antony and Cleopatra*. Did you see who put this card on your car?"

"No, that's the weird part—somebody set it there. Damn it, what I don't get is who is it meant for, Peggy or myself?"

"It's obvious to me that the person is a fan of Shakespeare," Marianne proclaimed.

"No, my damn luck. The weirdo is a play critic and wants to see us both thrown from the highest pinnacle and dashed to the ground in flaming fire."

"Now, who's being dramatic?" Susan said.

"No, wait. I remember reading an article in the newspaper a few months back. It was a story about a young woman. Oh shit, what did it say? I can't remember."

"No doubt, Peggy, you drink too much. We all know that!"

"No, something sounded familiar about the card on your windshield."

"Let me tell you, honey, this big city is dangerous. The other day my boyfriend, Robbie, and I were out on a date, and a group of guys threatened us. I'm unsure if it was because we were Black or gay."

"André, you wouldn't hurt a fly! Why on earth was someone threatening you?" Susan said.

"Now, all you bitches, listen to me. I want all of you to be on guard. Again, living in the city is dangerous. If you can't go out with a friend, don't go out at all!"

"Now, who's being melodramatic?" Peggy announced.

Returning the little card to Marsha, André said, "Look, child, whomever the card was meant for, take heed. I wouldn't go out at night! That's all I'm saying."

"Thank you, André. But you must realize that being a night owl is what we're all about. We're performers on stage. No one is interested in a matinee; that's only during

Christmas when the children want to see *The Nutcracker*!"

The waitress appeared with refreshments, and soon the mood changed; everyone told more joyful and humorous stories about who screwed up their lines on stage. Behind the smile, Marsha was still trying to come to grips with the strange reality that she and her friend were possibly being stalked.

Chapter 4

Weeks passed since they'd received the note on their car. Try as they did, Peggy and Marsha never ventured out at night without a friend in tow. However, the fear of the unknown danger soon faded as time passed. For Peggy, a newly discovered love interest mostly kept the two apart, and Marsha, no longer with a close friend to hold on to for comfort, found herself alone most nights.

After receiving bad news about her grandfather, Marsha returned home. After the funeral, a lawyer asked for her to come to his office. There she learned that her grandfather had a will no one knew about. It was his dying wish that Marsha inherited all his savings. The total amount, less than fifty thousand dollars, would be enough to buy herself a car and have some left over to deposit into her savings account for a rainy day, which was the norm for some working on Broadway.

When Marsha returned to her apartment in the big city, she found Peggy in shambles, crying on her bed. Her boyfriend had cheated on her with an understudy. Marsh comforted her friend Peggy, and the two stayed in their apartment the entire day without going outside. Nonetheless, since the show must go on, they found themselves that evening traveling down the busy boulevard toward Broadway for Peggy's next performance.

Their drive in Marsha's new car this time was a welcomed change. Finding a parking space always proved difficult. But, with determination, their efforts were soon rewarded with a spot not far from the building's entrance.

That night's performance was problematic because of Peggy's emotional attachment to the leading man. Still, Peggy was relieved to have her best friend by her side. She played her part magnificently.

When the show was over, they planned on meeting their friends for a celebration of sorts; the show was soon ending, and everyone would be going their separate ways to enhance their careers. Laughing and joking with one another, Peggy and Marsha left the Moore Theater in good spirits and hurried to get to their car before a cloud burst overhead. Unlocking the car, they hurriedly jumped inside.

But just as they departed, Marsha screamed, "What the fuck!"

"What's the matter?"

"Don't you see it?"

"See what?" Peggy shouted.

"The card!"

The two stared at the windshield and saw another gold card stuffed under the wipers.

"Damn, give me a minute," said Peggy. Getting out, Peggy grabbed ahold of the card, got back inside, and slammed the door. "Look, it's addressed to *Dear Someone*, just like before! Shit! What do you want to do?" Peggy asked.

"Well, look, we're already late. Let's take this note to the police in the morning. I'm not going through that bullshit again—for weeks, I couldn't sleep because of the last note we found, damn it," Marsha retorted.

"All right, I agree. We're going to the police station in the morning to file a report. Maybe they can find the weirdo writing this shit and have him arrested!"

"Arrested for what? Whomever, the wacko, is, they

never threatened us. But still, I hate these mysterious cat and mouse parlor tricks!"

"Me, too! I hate to ask. Do you suppose I should open it?"

"No freaking way!"

"Really—aren't you the least bit curious?"

"No. Hear me out. Let's meet our friends, have a goodbye celebration of sorts, and get stinking drunk! In the morning, we'll head to police headquarters!" Marsha proclaimed.

"I suppose. But I have to say I'm curious and want to know what this freak has written on his little card—"

"You see, that's what I mean!"

"What?"

"You don't even know if it's a guy that's written this. Have you thought it could be that bitch Deborah, the understudy who stole your Johnny?" Peggy suggested.

"Oh, come on. Don't be that naïve!"

"All I'm saying is curiosity killed the cat! Are you the cat?"

"Am I the cat? Jeez! Forget it. Look, we're here at the Pink Door."

They parked on the side of the building, then hurried inside just as it began to drizzle. A crowd was already standing inside, waiting to be seated.

"I hope André was able to get us a table," Peggy announced.

"Look, I see him waving. Come on, let's go."

Leaving the crowded entrance, the girls walked inside and joined their friends.

The joyful rest of the evening seemed a welcomed relief from the events of these past weeks. For Marsha, losing her grandfather was heart-wrenching—the man who had raised both her and her brother, Steve. Their birth mother, never the type to be a soccer mom, sought a life in the theater. As it seemed she was not one to control her passions, a couple of unannounced pregnancies were never a deterrent to becoming a famous star on Broadway—although that dream never materialized. She left her two children alone in this world, never knowing who their father was.

Peggy couldn't help but see Johnny and Deborah in the corner, smooching. She drank more than usual to aid her in the heartache but was soon relieved to see the pair of misfits leaving. Afterward, she grew quiet and didn't speak much.

On their way home, the girls spoke little, and when they arrived at their apartment, they hugged each other goodnight and went to bed, the promise of going to see the police still on their minds. For now, their lives were on a course that neither ever expected.

When Peggy awoke the following day, it was just past ten o'clock. She crawled out of bed and went to the bathroom to freshen up. A short time later, she returned to the kitchen and started the coffee. That's when looking through the bills; she spotted a note from the apartment manager.

Ripping open the letter, she began to read. *To all our tenants, we're sorry to inform you the rent will go up...*

Bla, bla! Shaking her head, Peggy crumpled up the letter and was about to throw it in the trash when she thought of Marsha. *Nope, before I throw it away, I had better let my roomie read it. Marsha is a stickler when it comes to financing. Speaking of Marsha, she's usually awake by now; she's usually the one making coffee!*

Peggy knocked on Marsha's door and said, "Hey, you awake yet?" She waited for a response but heard none. "Marsha, are you there?"

With still no reply, she tried the door. Finding it unlocked, she walked inside. To her horror, she found Marsha strung up, hanging from a screw-hook mounted in the ceiling, a hangman's noose made from wire wrapped around her throat, and a gag in her mouth.

"No!" Peggy screamed. "Oh my God, Marsha—not you!"

Frozen in place, unable to move, Peggy collapsed on the floor, crying. Nothing, there was nothing that could be done.

Now the reality of the gold card struck Peggy's thoughts. Was it an announcement of Marsha's impending doom that they chose to ignore? Were they too busy to heed the warning on their windshield? All this time, they should have contacted the police. Now it was Peggy's job alone; she would be the one who would make the call that should have happened before it was too late.

Chapter 5

Two detectives responded when the call came into headquarters. A seasoned Anthony Vargas and rookie detective Gunther Stevens appeared at the apartment building. There were already three squad cars at the entrance of the building with flashing lights.

Riding the elevator to the fifth floor, they stepped out into a crowded hallway where they heard weeping. There ahead stood the uniformed officers taking statements. Vargas flashed his badge and walked past the yellow tape with Stevens in tow.

Having grown accustomed to seeing what humanity could do to one another, Stevens found it better to focus on the crime scene and not the usual corpses lying in a pool of blood, staring back with open eyes wanting to know what happened to them.

Nonetheless, this situation was different. There, hanging from a piano wire, was the body of a young girl. Immediately noticeable was that she was fully clothed in her pajamas. But by the way, the bed looked, one could tell there was a struggle. The pillow lay on the floor, and the bedsheets and mattress pad were kicked off. Already her life had been cut short.

While they continued their investigation, Stevens noticed that the girl's hands were tied behind her back using duct tape, and a gag had been placed in her mouth. The gag was peculiar—he doubted it was a silk scarf.

Stevens left the bedroom and began searching the apartment.

This particular side of the building had no fire escapes. When it got dark, one could see the lights of Broadway off in the distance out the living room window. The windows were kept closed and secured.

Not surprisingly, the CSI team showed up and began their investigation.

Stevens, a friend of Marty Churchill, the youngest of them, greeted him with a wave. "Marty, when you search the girl's body, I want you to tell me what type of material the gag placed in her mouth was made from. I have a hunch it's not a silk scarf."

"Sure, no problem. Can do."

"Hey, Marty, did you see that basketball game last night? I thought Princeton would lose for sure. But no, they pulled off a win in the last two seconds!"

"I wish I did. But no, my youngest, Timothy, is teething, and the kid kept me up all freaking night. I'm beat!"

"Dude, you missed a hell of a game."

"I had taped it so I could watch it when I got home. Thanks for ruining that!" Marty responded.

A resounding laugh erupted from Stevens as the CSI investigator went to work, shaking his head in disappointment.

So far, in his examination of the crime scene, Stevens could find no forced entry into the apartment. On the north side of the building, there were no fire escapes to climb up. All the apartment windows seemed secured and locked tight. While Stevens considered how the killer gained access to the apartment, Marty appeared holding a plastic bag with a colorful fabric inside with the word EVIDENCE in red.

Handing it to Stevens, Marty said, "Well, I retrieved your gag—here, take a look. It's a pair of woman's silk panties. We'll take it to the crime lab and analyze it to see if there is any human DNA on the fabric."

"Is that blood on the panties? That's odd. You have to wonder what the sick-minded murderer meant by gagging this girl in this manner. Is there a message behind it, or was it simply a need that arose while the girl fought for her life and the killer gagged her with the only thing he could find?"

"That's why you get paid the big bucks, Stevens. You need to figure it out!"

"Yeah, the big bucks? Don't make me laugh! Hey, listen, I'm going to hold on to these and show them to the roommate."

"Okay, but why?"

"Let's just call it part of the investigation, shall we?"

"Sure, go ahead. I still have to take some crime scene photos. Look, sorry I ruined the game for you. It's still a hell of a game. You'll like it, I promise."

"All right, I will, thank you. Talk to you later."

"Until that time, old buddy."

Still contemplating how the killer got inside the apartment, Stevens met up with his partner and asked him what he had found.

After opening his notepad, Vargas read aloud, "The two girls were backup performers in Shakespeare's *Macbeth*. They have lived together for the past five years. Never a complaint about the living arrangement; they trusted one another up to the end. Recently, Marsha, the deceased girl, lost her grandfather and received a small inheritance. Otherwise, they were the typical starving artists you find on Broadway."

"Okay—hum, anything else?"

"Well, the strange thing was they received a note on their windshield a few weeks back. I have it and will let you read it when I'm done. But stranger than that: A few days ago, another note on their car was left that never got read."

"What do you mean, never got read?"

"Well, the first card upset the girls for weeks, so they refused to read another. It wasn't worth the time to open it and read what was inside."

"Where is the second note now?"

"The crime boys have fingerprinted it and marked it as evidence."

"Damn it, Vargas, what in the hell does the other note say?"

"We haven't gotten that far in our investigation yet. After the crime boys have labeled it and recorded it as evidence, we'll read what it says when we get back to the station."

"Calm down, son. You're getting into a tizzy for nothing."

"Yeah, okay, fine," Stevens announced, seemingly disappointed by his partner's reaction.

"So, tell me, did you discover how the killer gained access inside the apartment?"

"No, I haven't. I was about to go check out the bathroom and look there. From what I've discovered, all the windows and doors are locked."

Closing his notepad, Vargas announced, "There is something familiar about this case. There was another murder a couple of months ago that involved a girl receiving a card on her car. The detectives from Precinct 8 were working on the case. I remember something over the teletype saying the girl was strangled to death. I know the lieutenant at the station. Both he and I go way back to when we worked the streets together. I'll give him a call."

"Okay, let me finish up here. We can return to the station when I'm done."

"Sure, go ahead. I have some questions I want to ask the crime boys."

Walking into the bathroom, Stevens eyed the small space for clues. It was cluttered with an assortment of face cleansing products and makeup. The countertop had little room left. But what mattered most was the bathroom window. The killer could have entered the apartment that way if given any opportunity.

Nevertheless, the window opening measured only twenty-four by sixteen inches. It seemed pretty small. Black fingerprint powder was brushed throughout the frame's height and depth, which would hopefully give them the killer's identity if, indeed, he came in through the window.

Yet, after examining the window casing, it seemed nothing was disturbed. But on careful inspection, it appeared the window screen was installed backward. Inside the sink, the stopper was pressed close. Stevens eyed the assortment of makeup and hair products. Again, nothing looked disturbed, but the minor details and clues were there if one took the time to discover them.

Could it be that the killer placed his toes against the stopper and closed it as he stepped in through the window? From here, he could have fixed any small bottles he disturbed, placing them back into their original positions.

He imagined places the killer might have grabbed ahold of to steady himself. If he stepped into the sink, he would have to grab ahold of someplace else. Perhaps the towel rack or medicine cabinet?

Vargas appeared in the bathroom. "Hey, you ready to go?"

"Yeah, I suppose."

"Did you find anything?"

"I'm not sure, but I suspect the killer came in through the bathroom window."

"What! Like the famous song?" Vargas chuckled.

"No, never mind. I'll catch up with you downstairs."

"All right, hurry. I'm ready for a code 10-96."

"Me, too. I haven't eaten since this morning."

"Hey, it's your turn to pick up the tab. Don't forget!"

"Wait a damn minute. I bought dinner last time—why is it my turn again?"

"You lost the bet on the college basketball game, lest you forget!"

"Okay, I'll meet you in the car. I'll be down in a minute. I want to ask the roommate a few questions."

"Sure, go ahead, but I don't think you'll get anywhere. The roommate has taken a sedative and is in bed sleeping."

"No worries. I'll meet you downstairs. Go warm up the car, will you? I want to have a word with Marty, the CSI investigator. Just a hunch, but I suspect the murderer might have needed to hang on to something for support when they entered the house. Perhaps we might still get lucky and retrieve a print."

"I see Marty closing his tote box. You can tell him yourself."

Leaving the bathroom, Stevens saw Marty rummaging through his CSI tote bag.

"Hey, Marty, did you check for prints on the towel rack or medicine cabinet inside the bathroom?"

"Medicine cabinets, always. Towel rack, not so much. Why?"

"I believe the killer might have used the towel rack to brace himself as he crawled into the apartment bathroom window."

"I brushed fingerprint dust around it but didn't see anything. Let's go back into the bathroom to check."

"Hey, knowing you, you won't be able to rest unless we do. Let's go see."

In the bathroom, Stevens eyed the towel rack. Two sets of towels hung on the frame beside the washrag sitting in the middle. On the end of the rack, barely visible, the towel looked wrinkled. One could suspect it was moved out of place. Stevens, taking his pen from his shirt pocket, lifted the towel slightly, moving it out of the way.

"Marty, do me a favor and brush this area, will you?"

Removing the cap from the glass jar, Marty dipped a black brush into the powdered mix and brushed it across the metal bar. There he discovered a partial print of a man's hand. Unsurprisingly, there were traces of an unknown white powder, possibly from the killer's latex gloves.

"Good catch, Stevens. Although no plausible prints were discovered, we totally missed that one," Marty admitted.

"All right, we're done here. Let's go," Stevens announced.

When they arrived back at the station, there was a captain's note asking them to speak to them. Without hesitation, both the detectives appeared at their captain's door, where a small group of detectives was talking among themselves. Next, after hearing their names called out, Vargas and Stevens walked inside.

Detective Max Mulholland and his partner, Ben Holder, were there. Vargas asked, "Hey Max, what brings you to the 13?"

"That's the reason why we're all here!" Captain Hillsborough announced. "I'm afraid we might have a serial killer on the loose."

"Aww, shit," Vargas said. "I was hoping this murder

we were investigating wasn't one of those!"

"We're all going to a task force meeting in ten minutes. I've notified the chief's and the mayor's offices. They're sending someone down for the conference—should be here any minute."

"Tell me, Vargas, did you guys find a gold card on the murder victim's car windshield?" Max inquired.

"The strange thing is, according to the roommate, they've received two gold cards. One, initially a few weeks ago; the second, they never opened to see what was written inside."

"Listen to me, Vargas, I need those cards, do you hear me? It's important to our investigation. We must know what we're up against!" Hillsborough said.

Vargas turned to his partner.

Stevens shouted, "I'm on it!" and walked away.

"I wanted to ask you, Vargas, were your cards written as a poem, with the ending from a Shakespeare play?"

"Yes, it didn't make sense to me when I read it."

Stepping forward, Ben asked, "What about the location of the victim's apartment? Did they live high up in a high-rise, say, the fifth or sixth floor?"

"Yes—in the last murder, these girls were roommates for the past five years, never a fight or argument. They have lived in that apartment the entire time. High up on the fifth floor, supposedly where monsters couldn't reach them!"

"You see, Max, it just proves my point. What we have here is a trapeze artist or someone not afraid of heights."

"Yes, yes, I suspected that all along."

A small group arrived in the office: the chief of police, someone from the mayor's office, and two newspaper reporters.

The captain said, "Excuse me, Chief, but I thought we weren't going to have a news conference until after we had our briefing in the control room?"

"That's right. I invited the press as observers. Afterward, I'm to give a speech about our investigation and the possibility we have a serial killer on the loose," Chief Barns broadcasted.

While walking into the room, Stevens said, "I have the cards!"

"Perfect. Now let's get our butts to the conference room. The quicker we get the word out to the public, the sooner we can catch this guy."

"Excuse me, Chief Barns, are you saying a killer is a man, not a woman?" the young attractive blonde reporter asked while taking notes.

"No, I didn't say that. Please don't quote me yet! Mrs. Parker, we presently have no idea who the killer is. But you have my word; We'll catch whoever is responsible for slaying these young women. Now, if you'll excuse me, we have a conference to attend."

As quickly as they appeared in the captain's office, they all left following the chief, past the elevators to the back of the building, where a packed room of detectives and uniformed police officers had gathered.

When the chief and police captain arrived, the room fell silent. Now with everyone's attention drawn forward, the details of the two murders were made known. Copies of the two cards were xeroxed and magnified to ten times their original size. Next to them were pictures of the victims. They were similar: blonde women in their early twenties.

Besides the pictures, facts were written on the board describing further details—such as the proximity to where the two victims lived to one another, the streets and intersections where they parked their cars, places they worked, and their acquaintances and friends.

Standing at the podium, the chief tapped the microphone with his finger and said, "Good morning, everyone. Please, may I have your attention?"

The room fell silent; you could hear a pin drop.

Looking over at the printouts on the poster board, Chief Barns announced, "Precisely at 10:25 this morning; we received a call of homicide over at the Rigley apartment building. There was a young girl hanged from a piano wire. From what we could tell, it seems the killer entered the apartment through the bathroom window.

"Once inside, he placed a screw hook into the ceiling while the victim slept in her bed. Next, the killer woke the girl by gagging her with dirty underpants. Unable to resist, the killer bound the victim with duct tape, wrapped a noose around her neck, and hanged her like a piece of meat."

"Chief, could you tell me about the girl's roommate? Why wasn't she murdered?" Segreant Buckley asked.

"It appears the killer was only interested in the one roommate. When the card was placed on the car's windshield, it was unsure whom it was meant for—the victim or the roommate."

Stevens walked up to his captain and whispered something in his ear while handing him the plastic evidence bag. The captain whispered something to the chief, who grabbed the plastic bag. Then the captain sat in the next available seat.

The chief, holding the evidence, returned to the microphone and said, "I have just been informed another card was placed on the windshield that was never opened. Here today, we shall see what's inside. According to the roommate, the victim was so disturbed when she got the first card that she refused to open this card."

He was assured that it was adequately examined for fingerprints and any other evidence that could be collected.

The chief ripped the plastic seal, removed the card, and stared at it briefly. Next, he spoke into the mic and said, "It's addressed to *Dear Someone*."

Chief Barns read the contents to himself, then shoved it inside his pants pocket without any explanation. Instead, he continued discussing the need to watch out for suspicious characters.

Next, he turned to the captain and said, "Captain Hillsborough has more details. Stay sharp on your patrols—men, we have a killer loose in the city. Hillsborough, please." Stepping away from the podium, the chief said nothing else.

"Right!" Hillsborough announced.

The captain grabbed a marker and began to draw small-scale drawings of the city's street intersections. When he was finished, he said, "All right, all of you, listen up! These murders took place in a three-block section of the city! So far, we know that the first victim died in her apartment on 2nd Avenue, near Pike Place. The other victim, who worked at the Moore Theater on 2nd Avenue, lived a few blocks away. She was murdered in her fifth-story apartment. The victims' places were both in high-rise buildings—the first on the seventh floor and the second on the fifth floor."

"Cap, tell us, how did the killer get inside the apartments? Did he burst the door down?" Lieutenant Andrews asked.

"No. So far, all we know is that the killer was able to crawl up the side of the buildings. None would suspect that someone would be capable of crawling through such a small window as they did.

"The first victim owned a cat and allowed it to come and go on its own through a patio door left open. But this latest victim had no cat! According to the roommate, they left the small bathroom window open to allow for the steam from their showers to escape."

Captain Hillsborough signaled a uniformed officer, a young rookie officer named Amber. "I have asked our newest officer to hand out a bulletin to each of you. Inside the communiqué, you'll be able to read the details yourselves."

"Excuse me, Cap, so from what we know, we have a serial murderer on our hands then. Is that correct?" Sergeant Abbott asked.

"Yes, I'm afraid so. At first, we believed that Lillian Newburg was killed out of rage. Sadly, now we find that Marsha Krüger was hanged from a meat hook. According to what I've heard from Doctor Deborah Tremaine, the forensic psychologist, the first murder victim was killed by a disgruntled lover.

"Here is where things take a turn. The first victim was killed by manual strangulation, making the murder personal in nature. A wire hanged this second target. The killer could not have felt any exhilaration as they did with the first victim! She, I'm sorry to say, must have suffered. The department and Doctor Tremaine believe the serial killer is changing tactics and growing more daring with each murder. From this time forward, we need to be on guard in our patrols and especially take the time to look up into the sky. This killer is not afraid of heights, that's for sure!"

"Thank you, Captain, Hillsborough," Chief Barns announced. "Now listen to me, all of you. We have a real sicko on our hands. Keep frothy out there, and let's catch this guy!"

Afterward, everyone was dismissed.

A homicide detective's job is never done, and soon the department's resources were spent on other slayings and murders in the city as time marched on. Over time the usual suspects were brought in for questioning, particularly those with a criminal record involving rape or other abuse toward women. Soon, however, the case grew cold, and over the next year, no other *Dear Someone* cards were discovered on innocent women's windshields.

Chapter 6

None would ever expect the Covid virus to affect the United States as it did. This horrible invader mingled and crept into the most protected places imaginable. It seems there was nowhere to hide. None was immune, including the doctors and nurses on the front line. Apart from this, the police force had casualties of its own. One such detective named Vargas had been exposed to the virus and died alone in the hospital. Still, crime in the city never rested. Stevens was soon partnered with a rookie named Matthews, who, unfortunately, was exposed to Covid by his wife, who worked at a grocery store and had been quarantined for the past ten days, expecting to return to work tomorrow.

Gunther Stevens had been spending time on a case involving the murder of a pregnant woman engaged to a man who testified that she accidentally fell to her death when they were hiking the mountains. After reviewing the case file, Stevens suspected the fiancé from the start—especially when it was discovered that he was upset with the news of his fiancée being pregnant. He only had a year before graduating from medical school to become a doctor.

Opening his desk drawer, Stevens pulled out a familiar-looking gold card. Removing it from its protective plastic bag, something he'd done a hundred times before, he began to read what was inside.

Dear Someone,
I realize you don't know me. Listen to my words, you stupid bitch.
Regardless of your opinions, the stalker is close by, near death's door. Soon I'm afraid he'll want everything and more! O horror, horror, horror! Tongue nor heart cannot conceive nor name thee!
Signed,
The Eyewitness

This card was what Chief Barns read to himself that day many months ago. After reading it, he thought this card couldn't be from the murderer but someone trying to warn the girls that someone was stalking them. Stevens believed the word was out on the streets, and from the time of Marsha Krüger's death, no one had seen another. Whoever wrote this card must have seen the killer. It is a fact, in and of itself, but why wouldn't they come forward as witnesses?

His thoughts were interrupted by his new lieutenant, Jack Roberts, appearing at his desk.

"Stevens, I want you to come with me. You haven't had lunch yet, have you?"

"No. No time, I'm afraid."

"Good, lunch is on me. Come on. I'm buying today."

Following Roberts out to his car, Stevens hopped inside. On the way, he looked up at the lieutenant and said, "All right, come out with it. What's up?"

"You already guessed, huh?"

"Yeah, unfortunately, I fear you have something to tell me that is not good."

"Yes, you're right, I'm afraid. Your partner,

Matthews, has just lost his youngest daughter to Covid. He just called to tell me the news."

"That's bullshit, damn it, such a beautiful family and all. I'll call him when I get back to the station. Damn! Losing a kid is rough!"

"That damn virus has taken a lot of good people. Look, with morale at the station, I thought I'd take you out to lunch and give you the news myself."

"I appreciate that, Lieutenant."

"Look, we're here at the Tin Cup restaurant," he said, parking in an available space on the boulevard. Roberts reached inside his glove box and removed his face mask. He turned to Stevens and asked, "Do you need one?"

"No, I'm fine; I have a couple in my coat pocket."

"Yeah, it's a pain, but what can we do, right?"

"I agree. It's better to be safe."

Slipping on their masks, the two men exited the cruiser and walked inside. Once they walked past the doors, they stopped near the counter. The sign read: *Please seat yourselves in the places without an X.* The lieutenant grabbed a couple of menus, handed one to Stevens, and walked past a glass door to where the restaurant had patio seating under an awning. Being a sunny day, one had to take advantage of the weather. Mostly gloomy and cloudy, this place they call Seattle.

In their chairs, they had a perfect view of the city walkway. There, as if watching a movie, the picture constantly changed. Not far away, a man sat playing the guitar, his guitar case open for those to deposit coins.

Across the street, a man started his motorcycle; his loud exhaust pipes alerted every one of his intentions to depart. Not far from him, a young lady was playing the violin. She, too, had a case open for donations. With her was a girl singer wearing a mask.

A young waitress greeted them at their table with a friendly smile. "Good afternoon," she said; she, too, wore a mask. "Would you care for something to drink?"

Roberts said, "Yes, I'll take an unsweetened ice tea."

"I'll take a Coke," Stevens said.

"Stevens, if it's all the same to you, I already know what I want to eat. Do you care if I order now?"

"No, go ahead."

"I'll have a bowl of your delicious chili, smothered in onions."

"Chili! I'm not that brave. No, thank you. Please give me a cheeseburger and fries, thank you."

Taking the menus, the waitress disappeared.

When she walked away, Stevens, still disturbed about his partner's child's death, responded, "I still can't believe Matthews lost his daughter."

"I find it disturbing that all police departments throughout the city have been losing good men and women due to this virus. There is talk about a vaccine coming out by the end of summer, but how many people will be dead by then?"

"I know what you mean. Still, the virus hasn't affected crime in our city; it's still alive and healthy."

"So true, so true."

The men watched the public display on the sidewalks, and the conversation grew quiet. Soon the waitress brought their drinks.

Thanking her, Roberts asked for some cancer-causing sweetener and laughed.

The waitress smiled and said, "I'll be right back. I see your lunch orders are up."

She returned a few minutes later. The lunches were carried on a large plate. Placing the food on the table, she asked, "Would you like anything else?"

"No, thank you. I think we have everything we need," Roberts replied.

After she walked away, Stevens looked about the table and announced, "Damn it, I forgot to ask the waitress for ketchup!"

"No worries. Look, there's a fresh bottle on that guy's table. I'm sure he wouldn't mind letting you have his bottle."

Sitting at the table alone was a guy nursing a half-empty beer in a lead glass mug.

Stevens eyed him briefly and said, "Hey friend, do you mind if I take your ketchup?"

No answer. The man completely ignored Stevens altogether.

"Hey pal, do you mind if I take the ketchup?"

Still no answer.

Looking over at his lieutenant, Stevens shrugged, upset about being ignored. Next, he prepared himself for a confrontation with this cop hater and was about to stand when the waitress appeared.

"Oh, you have to forgive Andy. If you look closer, you'll also see that he lost his left arm. He lost his hearing in Afghanistan when an IED exploded under his vehicle."

"Oh, sorry about that, Andy," Stevens replied.

Andy turned and scowled at the two detectives as if he understood that the strangers were discussing his condition.

Ignoring the angry expression, Stevens turned back to the server. "Could you bring me a bottle of ketchup, please?"

"Yes, of course."

The waitress grabbed the bottle from Andy's table, placed it in front of Stevens, and said, "Here you go. Again, if you need anything, just holler."

"I have everything I need now, thank you."

After lunch, as they were leaving, Stevens stared down and watched this Andy drawing a picture of a group of people standing in a room in a medieval setting. Although the details of his drawing weren't made clear, Stevens thought he'd seen this background before.

For now, this Andy needed a bath. By his shabby clothing, he appeared homeless.

Hearing his name called, Stevens looked up and saw Roberts standing by the door, anxious to leave. As Stevens joined him, he glanced back toward the vet. There he saw society walking past the man that gave so much. None would guess that Andy had paid the ultimate price for America's freedom. Now he was a man lost in his art, with nowhere to call home.

When they arrived at the station, Stevens thanked Roberts for lunch and returned to his desk. There he saw several messages that needed his attention. He picked up the phone and dialed the first number on his list—the crime lab!

Stevens wanted to know about the analysis of some hair fibers they found in the trunk of a fiancé accused of murder. While waiting for them to pick up, he stared at the small card he'd forgotten to put away. He saw a small minuscule indention in the paper itself.

The crime lab speculated that the reason for the impression was from being held by a jeweler's vice or some other instrument. Now, something was becoming apparent, and Stevens quickly put it together—and then it hit him like a ton of bricks.

This Andy, the army war vet. He's the witness to the murders the newspapers have identified as the Romeo homicides!

"Fuck Me!" That got everyone's attention.

Lieutenant Roberts ran out of his office, looking

around to see what had happened.

Stevens shouted, "It's him, the witness to the Romeo homicides! He was right there the entire time, hidden under our noses!

"Who?"

"Andy, the army vet back at the Tin Cup restaurant. Come here, look closely at the card. See the small impressions? They're not from a jeweler's instrument but from the pinchers on his prosthetic left arm, which he uses to steady his writing!"

"What are we waiting for? Let's go. Now," Stevens announced.

"Okay, yes, I'll grab my coat!" Roberts said.

After meeting Roberts in the motor pool, Stevens quickly got inside the running car. No time to waste. They sped away from the station and hurried downtown. Something that couldn't be helped was the lunch traffic as many business employees were returning to work, making it more difficult to travel down the busy streets.

On the way, Roberts questioned Stevens on the probability of the cards' marks being something other than this Andy.

Stevens stayed to his guns and said, "No, I've stared at that damn card for months and only concentrated on the writing inside. I never considered the outside as being something special. It wasn't until today that I saw the card in a new light. I saw something so minuscule that it could have been easily overlooked. No, I'm sure this Andy is our witness. We must hurry!"

It took close to an hour to reach the eatery. With lights flashing, they parked out front and hurried inside. When they arrived, Stevens ran outside to the patio, searching for Andy. When he passed through the glass door, he saw where Andy was sitting was now abandoned.

"Damn," he muttered.

Looking around, the familiar waitress that had served them earlier was delivering a young couple their lunch bill when she saw the panicked expression on Stevens's face. She approached and said, "Can I help you, sir?"

"Yes. Do you know where this Andy had gone? The guy with the ketchup bottle? I need to speak to him at once."

"If you don't mind me asking, why?"

"Okay, yes." Removing his detective badge, Stevens flashed it to the waitress and said, "It's police business, you understand. Listen, I must speak to Andy at once. Do you know where he's gone?"

"Humm, I'm afraid that's a bit of a pickle."

"What do you mean? I don't get it!"

"Hey, listen, I have nothing against cops. But poor dear Andy, that's another story. You see, he looks homeless, right? The truth is when he returned from the war and was released from the VA hospital, he waited for his wife to show up. But sadly, she never did. After taking a taxi to his house, he walked inside and saw everything was gone, including his wife and newborn child.

"There, waiting on the table, was the most dreadful Dear John letter. He got drunk afterward and passed out in the back alley, not far from here. Sometime during the night, he was awoken by some cops, and they roughed him up a little because he resisted. The next day he was released from jail, but that night's memory left him hating the police. I'm afraid he wouldn't help you even if you asked him nicely."

"Look, I can't speak for everyone in police uniform, but I need to talk to him. Can you tell me where he likes to hang out or sleeps?"

"Andy usually makes his rounds in any number of bars

throughout the city. Do you remember last winter when we had that snowstorm? Well, Henry, the owner, knew he was sleeping under the freeway overpass. Instead, he paid for him to stay in a hotel room for a couple of nights. That's all I know. Sorry, I wish I knew more, but I don't!"

"Thank you. Tell me, what did you say your name was again?"

"I'm Penelope—Penelope Mikos. You can call me Penny—I'm always here, easy to find. I don't have a life, you understand." She laughed.

"I'm grateful for your help, Penny. Here's my card. If Andy shows up, please call me, will you?"

"I will, yes. But please promise me you won't give the guy a hard time, okay? He's suffered enough, believe me."

"I promise I won't hassle him."

Turning back to see Roberts, Stevens said, "Lieutenant, are you ready?"

"Sure. Nothing else to be done here."

Turning back, Stevens said, "Penny, before we go I want you to know this is a murder investigation. If you can think of anything, no matter how insignificant, please call the station and ask to speak to Lieutenant Roberts or me, Detective Stevens. We must speak with this Andy."

"I get it, really. Hey, wait a minute, you're not saying Andy is a murderer, are you?"

"No, nothing of the kind. But please get in touch. Please call if you see anything!" Roberts said.

The detectives got inside their car and drove away. As they turned down Broadway back to the station, their vehicle soon melded into the heavy traffic flow, leaving the congested area. Unbeknown to them, their visit to the café bar hadn't gone unnoticed. Earlier, this police cruiser had screeched to a stop, with lights flashing brightly, catching everyone's attention.

Hidden in the shadows, observant eyes had been studying their movements. It was Andy, watching and scrutinizing their return to the bar.

Andy studied the hooded strangler from a secret location, hiding in plain sight. He, the suspected killer, was performing his little act on the street, holding out a tin cup and begging for money.

What was unexpected was the sudden pause in his performance. Somehow, he understood he was being watched. No, not by his spectators tossing him change, but by Andy.

He was standing there, perfectly still, as patrons labored to drop change in his tin cup, his attentive gaze studying Andy's hiding place. Andy's immediate thoughts ran through his head: *How could he know that the Shakspearian artist and witness to his crimes was observing his performance? Indeed, unless this particular killer has been infused with cognitive abilities from the devil himself? Regardless, time to go, time to run—hurry, Andy. The beast is watching you!*

Chapter 7

Any homeless person has hiding places from the view of the public. Andy had his secret spots to sleep. Many dilapidated buildings in and around the city gave easy access to the homeless looking for shelter from the cold. Still, if you got caught, you'd be arrested for trespassing, spend a few nights in jail, and then be released back into society to starve and survive. Although things were different for Andy, he'd continued to hide from the police and that "freak show," making his living on the streets.

He debated going to the police but couldn't bring himself to trust them any further. Nonetheless, the strangler seemed to pick another victim—and Andy couldn't resist warning the unsuspecting woman. However, his last attempts failed miserably. Now all of this was nothing but speculation on his part. He could say the circus boy was a serial murderer even though he'd never seen the guy hurt anyone or anything. But, in Andy's estimation, he was the perfect candidate.

The word on the street was that the homeless performer liked to be called the "Jackal." This Jackal has been making inquiries, according to Reggie, the guy who worked at St. Mary's—a place he could count on to be fed. Reggie got word that the Jackal had been asking about the homeless vet he nicknamed the "Poet." But Andy's gut told him this Jackal character was up to no good.

There he goes, the Jackal, moseying down the crowded

sidewalk without a care in the world. Andy thought from his perch on the second story. *Wait, what have we got here?*

The Jackal stood frozen, backing inside a small crevice between buildings.

Someone or something has caught his attention. Then Andy saw the reason for the Jackal's pause. Half a block away, an attractive young lady was carrying bags to her car.

Yes—I see you, Jackal. What are you up to? As Andy stayed hidden in the upper room, looking out dirty windows, he didn't dare clean a spot so he could stare out. No, never be that stupid as to give away your location. *Damn, am I the only one that sees this weirdo? Look at him so tranquil and coy.* He was now hidden in the shadows, observing his mark. *The girl must be warned; she must understand she's in danger. Take notice of the car, get it right, always right.*

Who receives the note? Andy studied the pink Volkswagen. *Why do I bother? No one pays me any mind, especially when the killer is only a few feet away, and I've warned them. They continue with their lives—these beauties from the city ignoring my warnings.*

Now it seemed this Jackal found a new quarry to his liking. *Take note of the car. What year is it? The make and model? All this to get it right; get it right or else!*

Andy was urged to leave the hiding place, like the driver of the car speeding away, for one last look to check on the clown. *Where has he gone? Wait, not time to show himself. Oh, there he is. Look, I see you slowly emerging into the light, slithering like a snake. Now exemplary movements, looking behind, ever watchful. Promptly among your own, the circus act begins anew.*

Andy sat on the dirty floor to go through his belongings. He had his assortment of pencils and coloring charcoals in a small wooden cigar box. Soon he began to imagine what to say, how to give this stranger a warning. *Tell her that she's being watched. More than watched—danger. She's in trouble.* And so, it begins.

Dear Someone.

I realize you don't know me. You probably think this bizarre.

Regardless of your sentiments, the stalker is not far. Look now, from behind; he will appear. Hear my soul speak: / The very instant that I saw you, did / My heart fly to your service.

Signed,
Troubled

Perfect as before, this warning was to be on alert; there was a Jackal in the camp. Now all that needed to be done was to deliver this warning.

Looking out the dirty windows and dimmed light, Andy recognized that it would soon be dusk. He still hadn't eaten and had to go to the church before the line for the free evening meal was too long.

Andy didn't have much time to eat something and walk all those city blocks for the evening performance of *Macbeth*. Although the new actor playing Macbeth was a little flat—perhaps the guy had stage fright—Andy couldn't complain; after all, this theater was the only place in town with a Shakespeare play.

Andy gathered his heavy coat, personal belongings, and drawing pencils that he kept in a plastic bag. He would store the heavier items in his grocery shopping carts, such as his filthy blankets and sleeping bag.

Andy crept downstairs to the lobby of what once was a bank or some other financial institution. Since the last earthquake, this half of the building still lay in ruins. Yes, the chain-link barrier kept everyone out. Still, with the right tool, one could easily cut the wire fasteners free and pull the fence out to slip underneath.

Now he was outside under the usual weather conditions—rain and wind blowing in from the coast. Here it was always gloomy and cloudy, even during the summer. The estimated rainfall in Seattle is over thirty inches annually; one never knows when a rainstorm will appear. Shivering slightly, Andy slipped his coat over his neck and marched off to get fed, pushing his squeaky cart ahead of him.

When he arrived, he saw a couple walking their dog across the street. The dog barked wildly upon seeing him appear. Quickly pushing his cart, he turned a corner down the road to escape the annoying mutt. Now, ever cautious, he continued looking around him. By now, most of his fellow homeless citizens were already at the many churches offering hot meals and feeding those who showed up.

He emerged at the busy boulevard where St Mary's Catholic Church was across the street. Already the line out back had formed and was growing longer by the minute.

Just as he was about to cross the street, something caught his eye, and he rushed back into the shadows. As he observed something across the street, partly hidden behind a tree, Andy sensed movement. The lamppost not far away only gave off a dim illumination—not too bright and hopefully dark enough to hide his presence. What mattered most to him: Was he seen?

Andy watched to see if his suspicions were correct. Then the unexpected happened—the Jackal lit a cigarette. There, in the shadows, a flicker of a match. A split second later the burning match was blown out, the detailed image of the man and the red glow of the cigarette tip glowing hot. The creature slithered, a puff of tobacco in the air, then went back into the shadows. Who was he waiting for—could it be him? Why him? Why, indeed, was he on the Jackal's radar?

Andy ignored the sounds of disgust as pedestrians watched him crawl on the sidewalk. He retreated from the intersection and crept backward. Now to get away—run if he must—back to the bank, back to safety, hidden from view. *Leave now!*

When he reached the bank, he turned the corner and headed to the back of the building where the chain-link fence was located. At the spot where he entered the building, a police cruiser was parked there. Looking into the building, he could see two distinct flashlights shining in the darkness.

Andy sat on the wet asphalt and pondered what it meant. Did someone see him enter the building and report him as a trespasser? Or did one of his cronies follow him and discovered where he slept at night? Jealous of his subtle digs, they perhaps called the number on the fence, reporting the trespasser. One reality immediately came to mind: It would be a cold night.

Few choices were left to him. By tomorrow he would have to scout the city and find a new place—but where? Besides, the Jackal was on the loose, lest he forgot. Why would he be asking about him? Why indeed? A thought burst into his head: The Jackal must have seen him placing the cards on the dead girls' windshields.

Oh no, oh heavens no! Shit. I thought I was clever, believing I was washing the cars, acting like a fool! In desperation, he sighed.

After several minutes he grew hungry. Few options were left to him at this time of night. Still, he felt that searching some trash cans might yield favorable results, most often in cases like these—why he could eat like a king if he chose the right Seattle restaurant.

Still again, he asked himself, *why am I being hunted? Regardless, finding someplace secure where I can feel safe is best. I'll see Penny at the Tin Cup, and if I plan it just right, I'll get some tasty leftovers from the trash! I better check how much money I have, especially if I hope to buy myself a beer and have a dollar tip for Penny.*

Rummaging through his plastic bags, he found his hiding place where he stored his money but saw the loose change. *Not enough*, he thought. *Wait, Patrick was giving blood this afternoon. He should be recovering at his home under the overpass. Quickly go; he owes you for the last bottle you shared with him.*

Regrettably leaving his once-happy home, Andy scuttled away, pushing his grocery cart. Past a freeway onramp, he hurried through some brushes and over a rolling hillside near the massive concrete towers.

When he arrived in the darkness, he made his way to Patrick's cardboard shelter. As expected, when he crawled inside the small space, Patrick and Harper were enjoying a delicious bottle of Thunderbird. Harper was a guy Andy didn't particularly like. The reason was apparent—he didn't believe it when he spoke of his tour in Afghanistan when an IED exploded. Instead, Harper argued that he was in a car accident, not a hero overseas.

When they saw Andy, the look on their faces said it all.

"Hey dude, did you talk with that street mime over Broadway? He's looking for you." Patrick announced.

"What was that? Talk into my other ear—damn it, you know I can hardly hear out this ear. Besides, what do you mean some guy is looking for me? Damn, let me have a drink, will you?"

"Sure, have all you want. I was just leaving," Harper announced.

"Wait, what do you mean you're leaving? I just got here. What's up with you two anyway? You're acting strange, and I mean stranger than normal!" Taking the bottle, Andy unscrewed the cap and downed a couple of long swigs. Afterward, he handed it back to Harper.

"Patrick, I must say you're looking pretty good for a guy who has just given blood. You did give blood, right?"

"Funny thing about that." Patrick paused before finishing.

"Go ahead and tell him. Don't forget he's a war hero, remember?" Harper said spitefully.

"Sure, sure, let me have a drink first!"

Shaking his prosthetic left arm at Patrick, Andy shouted, "What have you done? Tell me now. Who gave you the money for this bottle?"

"It came from the mime. I had no choice; he wants to talk to you."

"I don't want to talk to that guy, damn it. Wait, wait a minute, did you say anything about where I was staying? No one is supposed to know about the crumbled bank building."

"Yes, I mean, he wants to talk to you bad. I didn't see any harm in telling him where you were staying. Look, he's not a bad guy—he bought me a bottle—right?"

"You stupid bastard, you know nothing! Give me the money you owe me. Do it now, or I'll beat your ass with my fake arm!"

Turning to Harper, Andy said, "Shut your damn mouth or else!"

"I don't have any money! If I had money, would I be sleeping here under the freeway?" Patrick exclaimed.

"Fine, you don't deserve this."

Andy pulled the bottle from Patrick's hands, what was left of it, then crawled out of the shelter and left in a hurry, angry that he was so quickly sold off for a cheap bottle of Thunderbird. Leaving the grassy hilltop, he walked back to the city. Finishing what little there was in the bottle, he tossed it in the bushes and considered his prospects. Things were looking desperate.

Regardless of the cops at the bank, I must find a way back inside, if only for one night out of the rain. But how could I? Besides, who in the hell does this mime think he is anyway? Why I eat circus freaks for breakfast, Andy thought.

Leaving the rainy freeway overpass behind, Andy walked down a dark alley and continued several blocks through the darkness, passing several busy intersections, back toward the Tin Cup, where he hoped to stay until closing. Remaining in the shadows, he studied the parking lot for some time, deciding on what he must do. This time, however, he would be trespassing if he was caught inside the gates. He froze and stared at the compact pink Volkswagen parked just beyond the fence at a tall, high-rise apartment building.

Still, he must deliver the note to the young woman; she was in grave danger and had to be warned. Andy pushed aside his concern for the petty crime of trespassing and couldn't resist the allure of attempting to save another unsuspecting victim.

The next victim. He believed a serial killer was on the loose, carefree, and brazenly killing as he pleased. There, a few yards away. He hadn't any choice; he had to act.

The parking lot seemed deserted, with no one outside. Most often, the public would avoid such weather and appear carrying their tiny umbrellas and raincoats long enough to scurry into the buildings or their cars. Here and now, all remained quiet.

There, just ahead, the unmistakable small compact, not like that other woman he tried to warn who lived with her friend. No, only one driver for this car! Still, if he placed the delicate paper on the windshield, he'd have to insert it into a plastic bag to prevent the rain from ruining it.

He paused next to a dumpster near a small enclave. The overhead light was enough to allow him to search his items for a plastic baggy. He found one once used for potato chips, with the greasy residue left behind.

Slipping in the signature warning card, Andy left his cart behind, crawled over to the small car, and stood erect while reaching for the wiper blade to place the card underneath.

Just as he did, he felt a cold, unforgiving wire noose wrap around his neck. Instinctively, he reached around to grab ahold of his attacker but was forced back into the shadows.

As Andy struggled to breathe, every move to free himself was met with a hard pull on the wire around his neck.

"I've caught you, my little songbird. Now the answers I've been searching for will be revealed. You, my friend, should have minded your business and let me alone. No, you couldn't, could you? All your attempts at saving my victims from my courtesies have failed."

"No one cares about you, a forgotten member of society, the homeless and least fortunate victims of this uncaring civilization. But my victims—oh, how sweet the words—my little screaming bitches, whose hope for another day of life ends inside the noose of my wire. To see them warned of danger and ignore the warning is more than I can bear." With a firm grip, the strand of steel never wavered.

"Sad, really, you pathetic little scamp. In the end, I suppose I should be grateful for your efforts at making the game more alive and thrilling. But no, you must recognize that the final bow is before us. Take your place on the stage."

The man's grip was overpowering, and Andy understood the tension of the wire around his throat. The one among us he desperately wanted to avoid had captured him. *How could this happen? How did I manage to get caught?* All these questions raced through his thoughts, but soon the world around him grew dark.

All the pain and hurt from being disfigured would not be more of an extended matter. Would he be missed? Would anyone remember him or his attempts at saving a life? Probably not. His final resting place was the crematorium—no longer the cold, rainy streets of Seattle but the hot oven to erase the life that once lived among them, the uncaring.

Jackal, you have murdered me!

Chapter 8

Shortly past nine in the evening, a call came to the police station. There was a report of a body found in the dumpster. Two homicide detectives were called out to investigate.

"Wait, I've seen that man before!" Detective Stevens said to his partner.

Standing inside the trash container, Matthews replied, "Stevens, what do you mean you've seen him before?"

"Matthews, look closely. I bet you find a prosthetic arm."

He stepped over the body and removed the stinky trash bags, some having already been ripped open, depositing their gross contents upon the body. Sure enough, a claw was attached at the end of the prosthetic arm among the rotting banana peels and TV dinner leftovers. Matthews tugged on it to free it but, regrettably, the body moved.

"Hey, it's still attached. But yes, you're right. I see it."

Stepping out of the dumpster, Matthews asked, "What can you tell me about the guy?"

"Well, other than he was a war hero reduced to being a homeless man living on the streets, not much else. I suppose he had a few run-ins with the police in the past and wasn't exactly obliging when it came to the Romeo murders. The CSI team has arrived. Trust me, we'll get more answers once they remove the body."

"So, what did you get from the witnesses? Anything

helpful?"

"Yeah, surprisingly. The man who found the body in the dumpster only went through the trash to find his daughter's retainer. It appears that most kids throw them away without realizing it, and if he hadn't been looking for it, we would have never found Andy's body."

"Andy, the victim's name?"

"Yes, we will get details once his body is removed. Then we can get the serial number off the prosthetic arm. I'm sure the Veterans Administration will have all the details on file."

"Did you finish interviewing the bystanders or possible witnesses?"

"Yes, the ones who came to watch the show. We still have to canvass the apartment building and go door to door."

"Wait a minute, did you see the shopping cart next to the dumpster?" Stevens asked.

"Sure, I assumed it was garbage from the maintenance man at the apartments that wouldn't fit inside the dumpster. Why?" Matthews asked.

"Not sure. Let me have a quick look. No, wait a minute. If I'm not mistaken, these are the personal effects of Andy, the guy in the dumpster. I see another pair of pants and smelly underwear. A shirt and something else—yes, a small cigar box!"

Stevens opened the box: Inside were Andy's sketches, pens, and loose change. "We better keep this; it could be evidence. One more thing—I don't see any security cameras around, do you?"

"No, probably couldn't afford the security cost. Older apartments such as these don't usually have cameras around."

As the two detectives talked, a uniformed officer

called Stevens' name. There beside him stood two cute young women.

Walking over, Stevens approached and said, "Yes, Officer, what is it?"

"This woman wanted to speak to you about some evidence she found underneath her car. It could be significant."

"Hello, I am Detective Stevens. What can I do for you?"

"Hello, Detective; my name is Patricia Harper. I'm not sure if this is important, but I found this strange note under my car. A friend and I were going to meet for a drink, but my car wouldn't start. It was frustrating. I had to call a tow truck—again. Well, as I waited for it to arrive, I called my friend Monica to give me a lift. The tow truck arrived and took my broken piece of junk to the shop. After the car was taken away, I found this note underneath my car. I'm unsure if it was meant for me or someone else, but here it is. Could you tell me if this killing is somehow associated with the Romeo murders? Oh my God—am I going to be the next victim?" The woman cried as her friend Monica held her tight.

Stevens, still wearing latex gloves, took the tiny note from Patricia, unzipped the used sandwich bag, and removed the small card. Immediately, he recognized the paper and the penmanship. As before, it was addressed to *Dear Someone*.

Dear Someone,

I realize you don't know me. You probably think this bizarre.

Regardless of your sentiments, the stalker is not that far. Look now, from behind; he will appear. Hear my soul

speak: / The very instant that I saw you, did / My heart fly to your service.
   Signed,
   Troubled

Stevens slipped it away inside his coat.

"It's the same warning, isn't it, Detective?"

"I'm sorry, but I cannot say."

"Shit, it doesn't matter. I'm leaving this damn city," Patricia muttered. "I told my parents about the serial murders here in town and promised that if I ever received a note on my car, I'd be gone in a New York minute. I'm out of here! Do you hear me? I'm gone!"

"Wait, we might need to contact you sometime in the future. You cannot leave."

"Listen to me, buddy. Write this number down. It's the phone number of my parent's house. If you need me, that's where I'll be."

Turning to her friend, Patricia said, "Goodbye! Sorry, Monica, I'm not going to stay. I'm leaving. No, not me!"

"But what about your job, car, boyfriend—all of that?" Monica said. "You cannot just walk away from the life you began here in Seattle to start anew somewhere else."

"Look into my eyes and tell me, if you were just told that death was knocking on your door, how long would you wait around to answer it? Tell me, Monica!"

"Not long, I suppose."

"Exactly." Reaching into her purse, Patricia grabbed her cell phone and dialed a number.

A few short rings later, a male voice was heard on the other end. "Hey baby, let me guess. Your car broke down!"

"David, oh my God, David. I'm the next victim of the Romeo serial killings."

"What the fuck are you saying? Slow down. You're

not making any sense!"

"Listen to me, darling. I'm leaving town and returning to my parent's house in the Midwest."

"You can't go! We have tickets for the game this weekend between Seattle and Minnesota. I bought these tickets months ago."

"Did you hear me when I told you that I'm to be the next victim of the Romeo murders? Did you freaking understand me?"

"Yeah, but babe, please listen. Why would someone target you? You wouldn't hurt a fly! I think it's all because of the murder movie we watched the other night. Besides, those tickets were pretty expensive!"

"Why in the hell won't any of you listen to me? I've told Monica and this detective I'm leaving town. But all of you refuse to listen to me."

"What detective? A real live cop?"

"You know what, David, you go and enjoy your stupid game. I'm glad to discover this selfish side of you that I've never seen before. I'm done. Have a nice life." Patricia hung up.

"Listen to me, ma'am," said Stevens. "This evidence you gave me is part of a murder investigation. In the future, we might have to contact you to testify. Again, we need you not to leave the city."

Ignoring Stevens' words, Patricia dialed another number, and immediately another male voice answered.

"Well, I told your mother we haven't heard from our daughter in a while and was beginning to worry."

"Daddy, oh Daddy, I need to come home," Patricia cried into her phone. "I'm going to be the next victim of the Romeo murders. Daddy, I don't want to die!"

"Wait a minute, honey. What are you saying now? Slow down and tell me what's wrong."

"Daddy, I found a note under my car. It's a warning that I'll be the next victim of the Seattle strangler!"

"Bullshit! No, that will not happen. You get home immediately. Do you hear me? Get home now!"

"I want to, Daddy, but this detective is telling me that I cannot leave Seattle in case they need me to testify or something at a criminal case."

"What detective? Put the man on the phone this instant!"

"Okay, here he is."

"Wait, what's going on? Why would I want to talk to your father? I told you already: You can't leave the city," Stevens objected.

"Please, Detective, talk with my father. I believe he'll have something to say about that!"

Grabbing the cell phone, Stevens said, "Hello, this is Detective Stevens. Can I help you?"

"Yes, Detective. I am Judge Harper from Abilene, Kansas. What's this all about telling my daughter she can't leave town? Before you say another word, I want you to know that I'm friends with your city prosecutor in Seattle, personal friends. Let's put aside this business and get my daughter back home to her parents. What do you say, Detective?"

"Yes, your honor, I'm sure we can arrange for your daughter to be put on the next airplane to Kansas if that's your wish."

"You got it, son. Thank you. I'm sure your department heads will recognize your efforts. Now please let me talk to my daughter."

Stevens handed the phone back to the hysterical daughter. He waited while hearing the sniffling agreements to get on the next plane out of town.

To his surprise, Patricia turned to him and asked,

"Detective Stevens, would it be possible for you to drive me to the airport? It's my father asking."

"Yes, that could be arranged. Yes, I'll have to talk with my partner, but I don't see a problem."

"Did you hear that, Daddy? The nice detective agreed and said he'll drive me there. What is that? A ticket will be at the customer pickup waiting for me. Wait, I still have to return to my apartment and get my personal belongings. But as long as I'm on that plane, I'm sure I'll be okay. What? Yes, of course, I'm shaken up. You have no idea, Daddy, what it feels like. Yes—see you soon. I love you. Wait, what did Mom say? I didn't hear her. Okay, tell her I'm coming home. Love you."

After hanging up, Patricia said, "It's all settled. I'm just waiting on you, Detective!"

"Sure. Listen, why don't you go to your apartment, gather your belongings, and meet me here when you are finished? Regrettably, I'm in the middle of my murder investigation and still have evidence to gather and eyewitnesses to question."

"So, you want me to go to my apartment alone?"

"Don't you have your friend Monica? By the way, where is she? I don't see her anywhere."

"While you were talking to my father, she told me she had to get home to her kid and didn't want to be late."

"Please go to your apartment, and I'll meet you there. Just tell me your number."

"Sure, okay, if you think it will be safe."

Stevens' partner called for him as they pulled the body out of the dumpster. "Stevens, you need to see this!"

"I'll be right there."

Stevens turned to Patricia to tell her that he wouldn't be long. But before he could, she was already stomping away toward her apartment to get her belongings.

Oh hell, she'll be fine. Shit, it's not even midnight—no monsters roaming this time of night, not yet, Stevens thought.

Turning back to his partner, he yelled, "I'm coming. Wait a minute."

As Patricia walked past the lobby, the apartment building looked deserted. Nothing to see here, inside the lobby—but outside, a dead man being removed from the trash dumpster, something to see for all the sick-minded shits. With no time to waste, Patricia wanted to get away as quickly as possible and pressed the elevator's call button.

The elevator seemed to take a lifetime. Of course, this apartment always had a slow elevator car that seemed to take forever to arrive, something the tenants had complained about often. To Patricia's relief, the elevator came, and—even more of a liberation—no one was inside. Hurrying in, she repeatedly punched the eighth-floor button. But when she did, the creaking doors did nothing. Seconds later, the carpeted doors closed her inside. After a thud, the cramped space lifted upward.

She had not traveled far when the elevator stopped on the third floor. Next, the doors swung open, and a guy wearing a black hoodie walked inside. Patricia took a long breath in disgust. *What now?* The stranger, who never bothered to look up, remained silent. He seemed distracted, more so than her. Gratefully, she saw the door close again, and the car ascended upward, but something was strange. The guy never punched a floor to exit. Instead, he stared at the floor.

Now, more than ever, Patricia became nervous and backed against the walls. She had no weapon, nothing to defend herself. Why was she so stupid as not to bring something to protect herself in case this weirdo went on the attack? She'd only caught a glimpse of the stranger—he looked young, with no wrinkles or facial hair to speak of. But could, she be sure? It was a quick look and nothing more.

The panic inside her grew to a fever pitch. Perhaps she should attack this guy. Be the first to draw blood; give him something to think about before he tries to hurt her. As if she could be so brave, much like in the movies. *How stupid.*

Now, more than ever, she wished she carried a knife or even a gun. *A gun—again, how stupid to think of such a thing.* David tried to get her to keep a weapon on her and often said, "These streets are dangerous, and no woman should ever be alone." *Oh my God! Now, who's sounding stupid now?*

Something about this stranger, something in the way he was standing. Then she realized: *He's not just standing; he's swaying. The guy is messed up; he must be on drugs or something.* Shit, an even more reason to be on guard. What if he wanted to rob her and tried to take her purse? What if he slit her throat? Now, more than ever, she wished she had gone to those exercise classes on kickboxing a punching bag.

She had been offered to attend in the past by Janice, but she was always busy with David. *Damn.* Maybe she could punch him in the face and run. *Run? Run where?* No, she wasn't going anywhere until that damn elevator door opened. *Shit!*

Looking soullessly at the stranger, she thought, *Don't think this will be easy, mister. At least I'm awake and won't make it easy for you. No pushover here today. You'll pay if you attack me. You'll die as I scratch your eyes out, you coward!*

Ding. The elevator came to a stop on the eighth floor. *Now, move your fat ass. Get your stuff.*

Being the first to leave, she hurried down to her apartment. She fumbled with her keys and unlocked the deadbolt.

Pushing open the door, she stepped inside. For the first time in a long time, or if ever, her apartment felt strange to her. Perhaps it was because she was cutting ties with the city and about to move on, or she no longer felt safe. Whatever the reason, she felt something was amiss. In haste, she flicked on the kitchen lights and cautiously looked around. Inside this place, she used to feel the safest. All was quiet; there were no sounds—just the eerie stillness.

On her countertop was a cutlery set, given to her last Christmas by her mother. Hurrying over to the counter, Patricia grabbed the giant knife in the bunch as if an attacker would burst out from the shadows at any moment. Gripping the long blade firmly, she again looked about. Then she yelled out something unexpected, even for her: "If you're here, I want you to know I won't go down without a fight—do you hear me, you bastard? I won't go. You'll have to kill me first. I have a knife, do you hear me? I have a weapon, and I'll cut your balls off, you son of a bitch. Stay away. I'm warning you!"

Afterward, nothing but the eerie silence, only disturbed by the occasional car horns down on the street below.

Damn it, Patricia, get your stuff and go.

Patricia took a step toward her bedroom, but a revelation appeared as she did. The patio door was open, noticeable by the curtain's swaying, blown open by the passing breeze. *Tonight. Think about this evening before you go down to talk to the cops. Did you open the patio door?* Uncertainty clouded her thoughts, which infused her nervousness. Her hands trembled. *Damn, how hard could this be? Think, did you or not?* She couldn't be sure.

She pointed the knife outward—the attacker would be the first to die if he did appear. Another thought: *Damn, what if there are two attackers?* Oh, no doubt she'd be screwed! Feeling one of those stress headaches, Patricia became angry because of her weaknesses. Her frailty as a woman didn't always have to be—no, the best man for the job was often a woman. *Really, a joke at a time like this?* she thought.

She couldn't figure out why the detective didn't bother to escort her to her apartment. Someone dead—in a trash dumpster, of all things. No, not just a dumpster but *her* dumpster where she lived. The note, yes, the message she found under her car. *Oh my God, was it written by the man in the dumpster or the killer? What does this mean? He killed himself and jumped in the trash? Come on, stupid, really! No, someone killed him. Wait, someone killed him while he was trying to place a warning on her car—the one that warned her she was about to die?*

As if a ton of bricks landed on her head, the reality she was to be the next victim struck her again profoundly. Near the door in the next room, there was another light switch. Feeling brave, she hurried into the bedroom and flicked on the light. Now, more than ever, it was time to leave; she felt it deep in her soul.

Racing to the bathroom, she flicked on another light; the neon lights above flickered and burst on brightly. She grabbed everything off her countertop, opened one of the drawers, then grabbed the overnight bag, shoving everything inside—all she could.

Next, she went to the medicine cabinet, only taking the prescription drugs—mainly the ones for depression, cough, and cold—and left behind her birth control pills. She raced into the next room. Setting the knife down on the bed, she ran toward the closet and removed a suitcase from the top shelf. She went to her cupboard, removed her underpants and bras, and tossed them inside.

Next, she opened her sock drawer, grabbed several pairs, and tossed them inside. Then she turned her attention to the clothes hanging on the rack, giving little attention to what was there. She grabbed three pairs of slacks, one pair of blue jeans, and two tops and tossed them all in. Glancing at the array of shoes she'd collected, she thought, *Leave it all for the cleaning lady—I'm sure she'd want them anyway. No more time to waste.*

She shoved everything she could inside the suitcase, including the overnight bag with her meds, and zipped it closed. A few items didn't fit. *Who cares?* What was on her mind most was to get out clean.

Grabbing the knife in her right hand, she took her suitcase and turned to leave. When she reached the door, a shadow flashed before the opening, out in the hallway.

Patricia froze in place and didn't move. She was trapped like a rat. There, beyond the door, was her freedom. She was trapped inside her apartment, which could be where she would be discovered dead.

With her eyes, she followed the movements of the shadows standing outside in the hallway, which moved and tilted side to side—*no choice but to make a run for it.*

If she could reach the hallway and scream out, perhaps a neighbor or someone would hear her and come to her rescue. Or she'd be dead, much like those two other girls.

Now, more than ever, she had no time to waste. Her opportunities were few, and she knew in her heart that there wouldn't be another.

She grabbed ahold of the suitcase, held it up to her chest, took the large knife in hand, ran toward the door— out of her apartment in the hallway—and made it out safe.

Unexpectedly, as she appeared outside her apartment, there to greet her was the guy in the black sweatshirt.

"Hey, my name is Robbie, and I was wondering if you are free this weekend?"

"What? Am I free this weekend? Robbie, you want to take me out on a date?"

"Yeah, I kind of have been checking you out. I thought it was time to ask you out. What do you think? Do you want to go with me and have a burger someplace? I hear McD's has a special all you want on the menu for just $5.99. Don't worry; I'm buying nothing cheap. You can have anything on the menu you want!"

Patricia stood there in the hallway, wondering about this ridiculous offer. She still held the large butcher knife in her hand. Ignoring his words, Patricia set down the suitcase and responded, "Please, Robbie, excuse me for a minute."

She ran into the apartment, placed the knife on the countertop, and returned outside. She needed to get out of town in earnest, and she didn't need a kitchen knife; it was unlikely she was going to make dinner for anyone.

"Now tell me again. What were you saying about a date?"

Fumbling over his words, Robbie began anew about getting a cheeseburger as Patricia glanced back into her apartment and back into her bathroom at the medicine chest mirror. She studied the reflection in the mirror and saw the shadow move.

Instantly grabbing her suitcase, Patricia yelled, "The killers are in my apartment!" The reality struck her profoundly, and she screamed, "Robbie, run!"

She bolted toward the fire escape stairs, down the stairway to the ground below, leaving Robbie in the hallway to figure out what he'd said to upset her—perhaps she was a vegetarian or something?

When Patricia arrived back at the parking lot, she ran up to Detective Stevens and screamed, "The murderer. He's in my apartment! Damn you, I told you. I tried to tell you, you stupid bastard. Hurry and get the man; he's hiding in my shower behind the curtain. Apartment number 8-12, the door's unlocked. Hurry before he gets away!"

Detective Stevens dropped everything and called out to his partner to join him. The two detectives quickly ran up the stairwell, back toward Patricia's apartment.

When they arrived, the door to her apartment was still open. All the lights were still on. Hurrying inside, the detectives began searching for the murderer.

Detective Stevens ran into the bathroom and pulled back the shower curtain. There, to his surprise, were dirty footprints—the impressions, the same as before, made for mountain climbing.

Stevens told his partner, "She was right, damn it. The killer was right here!"

"What is that you're saying? What do you mean the killer was right there?" Matthews responded.

"Come over here and check out the bathtub! The killer was standing right here waiting to pounce."

"Shit, man, I can't believe the balls on this guy; they must be made of brass. To be that bold and wait in the bathtub for his next victim."

"Yeah, this girl tried to tell us, but I didn't listen. Too damn interested in chasing the evidence."

"Well, the guy is gone now, right?"

"Yeah, listen to me for a moment. I have to drive this girl to the airport. Do me a favor and close her apartment door and lock it up—alright?"

Hearing no response, Stevens yelled, "Matthews, did you hear me?"

Leaving the small bathroom, Stevens walked into the living room, where he saw his partner standing near the couch, looking down at the floor.

Turning around, Matthews said, "We do have a body—a fresh kill. Look here, a guy with a kitchen knife sticking out his eye. The victim is still warm; the killer couldn't have gotten far!"

"You don't think the girl killed this guy, do you? The one screaming about someone being in her apartment?"

"No way. She's too scared."

"Where? How?" As Stevens' words left him, he saw something dark standing outside on the balcony. He reached for his revolver and screamed, "Stay where you are!"

Turning around, Matthew saw something dressed in black and gray—a set of tiny wings burst open—and whatever it was jumped out over the railing and flew away.

Rushing to the banister, Stevens was about to fire a shot at the strange dark object but knew better than to shoot at the suspect; a civilian could be injured along with his career.

"What the hell was that?!" Matthews shouted.

"I don't know but run. Let's get into the car and chase that fucking thing down. Look, do you see the direction it's traveling? It's heading toward the freeway. We're only eight stories up; it won't get far. Come on. Run, damn you!"

"What about the dead guy?"

"Leave him. We'll close the door. Come on. We must go, Matthews."

"All right, all right. I'm right behind you. Let's go."

Hurrying from the apartment, the two detectives ran down the fire escape toward the street. When they arrived, a frightened Patricia was holding her suitcase in hand.

"What did you see? Tell me, I must know!"

"Look, I cannot go into it now, but we gotta go. The killer is escaping!"

"The killer? So, he was in my apartment waiting, wasn't he?"

"Yes, yes. Do not go anywhere until we return, do you hear me? Stay right here!"

"What about Robbie? Was he there?'

"Who's Robbie?"

"A guy was asking me out on a date. I left him back at my apartment when I ran for my life."

"Damn it. We gotta go. Now!" Stevens yelled.

"I'll miss my flight if I stay here. Wait, I have a better idea—let me go with you. You guys can drop me off at the airport afterward."

"We don't have time to drop you off at the airport. We're on official police business, and you're letting the killer get away!"

"Why are you telling me this? How do you know he's a killer?"

"Wait, we don't have time to get into this now. Jump in my car," Stevens shouted.

Matthews said, "Hello, lady, we're wasting time! You heard my partner. We must go. Now!"

"All right, maybe this will help, or maybe it won't. But I rode with my brother back home; he's a cop."

"Move your asses. The guy is getting away," Stevens shouted, blowing his car horn.

They jumped in the car and, with Stevens behind the wheel, began to pull away but stopped near the CSI team. Stevens shoved the car into park and jumped out, calling the head investigator, Ziller. When the man approached, he ordered him to investigate Patricia's apartment, 8-12.

"That was our next stop after we finish collecting

evidence here," Ziller responded.

"Look, no time. We must go."

"We'll take care of it."

"Thanks, goodbye. Gotta go."

The car siren was ear-piercing as they sped away.

Chapter 9

No surprise, they lost sight of the flying Batman, or whatever they'd call it, with its lean dark body and wings. With no easy route to get to the freeway, the surrounding landscape was dotted with grassy hills, and the path to the highway was hindered by apartment buildings, fast food restaurants, and gas stations.

The police car hurriedly drove through the narrow streets as the flashing lights and siren alerted everyone to their presence—meaning, *Get out of the way!*

On the radio, Matthews notified dispatch to send other units to their location; a homicide suspect was on the loose. On a hunch and a prayer, they parked near an apartment building. The loud siren became silent, and the police lights were flashing.

Grabbing a flashlight from the car door, Stevens jumped out, with his partner, Matthew, directly behind him, carrying a shotgun. Patricia was ordered to stay in the car as the men ran off.

The sound of more sirens approaching filled the night air. A car came screeching to a stop only feet away. Another pair of cops jumped out and ran back to the other side of the tall shrubs on the hunt. Another car rolled up, and a single officer stepped out. Something was different in that this officer had a companion of the four-legged kind! Excitement and barking, all types of barking.

This K-9 knew he had a job to do and was anxious to

get it done. The officer slipped a leash onto the dog's collar, and the pair ran off on the hunt for the killer.

Inside the police cruiser, Patricia sat silently. This killer had stood in her shower, waiting to pounce and strangle her. The emotional scar left would not heal for many years to come—if ever. She physically shuddered at the thought—so close to death's door, so close to meeting the Grim Reaper.

Typical for Seattle, it began to drizzle. The streetlight was drab at best, giving off some light but not enough to make her feel safe. Now, however, she regretted her decision to have Detective Stevens drive her to the airport—the better plan would have been to call a cab. Still, she could call her old boyfriend, David. But as soon as he got the call, he'd no doubt begin with his arguments to make her stay here in Seattle. He'd suggest that Patricia could move in with him. No, her mind was made up; she was leaving. Today, tonight, as soon as these detectives came back!

Everything grew eerily quiet. Patricia sat inside the car alone, the water dripping off the car windows. Through the water streaks, she studied her surroundings. No one was there. Although a distance away, looking out the back window, she could see a gas station where customers filled up their cars. Still, so far away. None could guess that a killer was in the area.

Completely unaware of the danger, we dumb humans often go about our lives, never knowing the savage acts of cruelty played out under our noses. Patricia sat, thinking of her death in the papers. What would be the immediate reactions of her friends or coworkers? Not to mention her parents, damned to read about it in the newspapers or receive the phone call: *I'm sorry but your daughter is dead—just another victim of the Romeo Strangler.*

Alone in the back seat, Patricia hadn't noticed the different smells. She looked down at black floor mats, considering the previous occupants who had sat in this seat—drug dealers, rapists, drunks—all who seemed to leave their remnants of stink behind.

Patricia sat back against the seat and sighed. She was more than ready to leave. Growing anxious, she shook her head, thinking of what could be taking so long. Her patience was growing thin. She was staring out the window for any sign of the detectives: nothing outside, all dark and gloomy. *No, I'm afraid these cops missed their chance.*

The patrol lights flashed against the scenery as she stared out the window. *Where did everyone go?* Undoubtedly, the killer must have gotten away. *Damn, the monster flew away. Who does that?* Whoever this crazy bastard was, she hoped he would get caught soon. No doubt she'd be called upon to testify at the hearing, but to say what? She'd never seen the murderer. No use in testifying to something you never saw—right?

Next, she became cold. She was hoping to turn on the car engine and flick on the heater. She looked about at the front dash. *No keys, damn*, she thought.

Something outside caught her attention. In the shadows, something moved—right there, next to the tall scrubs that dotted the sidewalk. Something was there! Yes.

She froze in place. All around, her attention was concentrated on this one place and nothing else.

She watched for the slightest movement. Only a moment ago, there was nothing there. But, as if by magic, from the shadows, something slithered out. The shape soon came into view. But with the raindrops against the vehicle windows, she struggled to see.

There it was, the unmistakable tall shape of a man—all in black.

The dark object continued to creep out from the bushes only a few feet away. It had discovered her inside the squad car. How was it possible? *Damn it, where are the cops? Where's the K-9 unit?* The killer had stumbled onto her. There it was, afresh and new. It was bravely advancing— to do what? Kill her here and now?

Plainly in view, the monster stepped up to the squad car. Its face was partly hidden under a hood.

As Patricia watched, frozen in fear, it walked up to the car and looked inside. She leaned up against the opposite car door, tilting backward as far back as she could go away from the monster. She saw its face, now plainly in view, all painted in white, the outline of his mouth all black. Its yellowing teeth, against the white paint, were made more visible.

Leisurely, his hands, covered in black gloves, wiped away the droplets from the glass. Now, as they eyed one another for the first time, Patricia saw what would have been her last image of her killer. The crooked smile, the ghastly, long fingers hidden inside a glove.

Now nothing kept her from the killer's grasp. The reality, horrid reality was that the doors were still unlocked. A split second before the beast could rip the door open, Patricia punched the door locks, locking her safely inside the small compartment.

The killer jerked on the door, pulling on the handle. Thankfully, its attempts were unfruitful. As a result, it viciously punched the car's hood.

Next, to her relief, she heard a distant noise—a dog barking. The killer pointed its finger at her and smiled. No words were spoken; he ran away. Next, she heard a motorcycle starting up nearby. When the detectives arrived at the car, Patricia jumped out.

"You missed him!" she cried at the top of her lungs.

"How? What do you mean? Was the killer right here?" Stevens responded.

"Yes, he took off on a motorcycle not five minutes ago."

"Quickly, tell us. What did he look like?"

"Your worst nightmares come true!"

"No, his body type. Was he tall or fat?" Matthews responded.

"I wasn't looking at its body—no, look at the car window; it made an imprint on the glass with its fingers. The smile is painted on a clown of some type. I don't know; I hate clowns."

"So, it was a circus performer, you're saying?"

"No—yes, it could be, I suppose. Listen, I'm done with this. Please take me to the airport."

The K-9 officer arrived at the car, his dog barking constantly. "We'll get him next time, girl. Tell me, who's a cute puppy?"

The dog, in response, pulled the officer toward the squad car, sniffed around, stood still, and began barking again. The guy had been right here, standing next to the vehicle. Muffy got his scent.

"All right, where did he go? Show me, girl."

The pair ran toward where the motorcycle had taken off, followed by more barking. The team returned a short time later; the dog was let back inside the back of the police car and excitedly barked even more until given its favorite toy.

Afterward, the lone cop approached the two detectives. "From what I could tell, the suspect ran over toward the apartment carport, where it had an escape vehicle waiting, and took off. The dog lost the scent over there, just beyond the trees."

"Roger that! Okay, nothing else to be done. Thank

you, Officer Byerly. We'll contact you if we need anything else," Stevens said.

"Can we go now?" Patricia shouted.

"Yes, of course. Thank you for your patience," Stevens responded.

"What choice did I have, right? No matter. Please get me out of here, away from this city and its living nightmares."

"Fine. Get into the car."

Inside the vehicle, Matthews radioed headquarters and checked in. Then, after being told to contact the head CSI investigator, Matthews pulled out his cell phone, speed-dialed a number, and waited. A man soon answered. The news, not surprisingly, was that the dead guy in Patricia's apartment had been dead less than an hour. Distinct shoe impressions were left in the shower and out on the balcony—a man's size twelve. No fingerprints; the suspect must have been wearing gloves. Other than that, was some amateur cell phone footage—someone had caught the killer flying away.

"Not much, just a dark object in the sky," the CSI investigator finished.

"Thanks for the report," Matthews responded.

"What did the investigators find?" Stevens asked.

"I'll talk to you when we're alone."

"Roger that."

"When we get back to the station, we'll check out the video. Perhaps the lab boys could enhance the footage; it's all we got, although it seems we might finally have a break in the case," Matthews announced.

"I suppose. As you said, it's not much."

From the back seat, Patricia said, "I hope you catch that bastard. It needs to be exterminated. I cannot get the image out of my head. Damn, that thing was terrifying!"

"Well, face painting made to look horrible. I suppose it seems frightening to you, but we encounter all kinds of weirdos almost daily, believe me," Stevens spoke.

Gripping the suitcase filled with her worldly possessions, Patricia sat quietly for the rest of the trip. When they arrived at the airport, Stevens got out, walked to the back of the car, and opened the door. As Patricia jumped out, Matthews thanked her again for her help and told her how sorry he was that she had experienced such a horrible thing.

Patricia thanked Detective Stevens and said her goodbyes. When she closed the door, she looked at him and apologized for calling him a stupid bastard.

Stevens chuckled. "If that's all I've ever been called, I'll be surprised. No, I've been called far worse."

"You get it, right? I felt something was waiting for me in my heart, and I was right. Sadly, the hooded guy should have heeded my warning. Who knows? Maybe he saw something back in my apartment that he wanted for himself. Whatever it was, it cost him his life."

"Believe me, both Matthews and I understand. Now listen, put this behind you, and go home. Once you're there, the nightmares will fade over time. You're a beautiful young woman, and your future looks bright!"

"Thank you. I'll try. But there is one thing that bothers me."

"What's that?"

"What about the other girls?"

"What other girls?"

"The ones that this murderer will kill and destroy—what will happen to them?"

"I cannot say. But I can say that we will catch this monster and put him behind bars. For that, you have my promise. I believe he's getting sloppy. We already have a description and a photo. It won't be long."

"I hope you're right, I truly do. All right, I must go. You have my father's number. If you need me, please do not hesitate to call."

"We will. Goodbye, Patricia Harper."

With nothing left to say to the two officers, Patricia hurried inside the terminal to the Southwest Airlines ticket booth, where she gave her name. The attendant searched the computer and soon found a ticket already purchased. A short time later, she was given a boarding pass and told from what terminal the plane was leaving.

Going through the TSA checkpoint, she soon looked for a small café, someplace to eat a small bite. Now, for the first time in hours, she felt safe—safe from being murdered and all that craziness. The question that haunted her most was whether she would ever feel safe again. *How do you pick up the pieces and begin anew? What of the countless crime victims who wake up and start their days, having survived a dreadful ordeal? How can they?*

After finding her gate, she picked a place and sat next to the window. The plane had just arrived and was disembarking. Most of the travelers looked tired, perhaps feeling nauseous from the flight or the effects of alcohol they consumed to forget about the bumpy rides caused by air turbulence.

Nonetheless, the plane was refueled, the luggage made its way on board, and the lines to board the aircraft began. Patricia was surrounded by children crying and stressed-out fellow travelers who had no way of knowing how lucky she felt to be among them. She had been so close to dying, seeing her killer's reflection in the window. Those pair of hands were meant to strangle and kill. All this drama was a stark reminder of her mortality.

Something was taken from her inside that police car.

She felt robbed of her innocence—with no easy way to explain it.

The line of passengers made their way onto the plane, crammed inside like sardines in their assigned seats.

Soon the stewardess checked all seat belts. Minutes later, the plane, like a well-oiled machine, pushed away from the terminal. Again, rain poured across the windows. This time she wasn't alone—no, this time, others were with her. Still, she didn't feel safe.

The ride across the runway, the concrete below, the cracks were felt by everyone, but then they were suddenly coming to a stop. The plane waited behind others waiting to leave, with the smell of jet fuel inside the cabin. Next, the pilot came on the overhead speaker, telling the stewardess to prepare for takeoff.

The plane took its place, ready for departure. The passengers sat and chatted among themselves over the sounds of the tested jet engines.

The concept of flying planes defied all natural weight realities—something so heavy could never fly. However, engineering said otherwise; the plane rolled down the runway and soon experienced lift and thrust, then rose into the night sky.

For Patricia, while experiencing the slight turbulence, the flight took on new meaning and flew to an altitude of over forty thousand feet.

When Patricia's flight landed in Wichita, Kansas, she hurried off the plane; she had chosen not to check any bags. All she had she held in her hands.

Patricia arrived at the airport lobby, and there to meet her were her mom and dad.

Collapsing into their arms, she cried bitterly. During the flight, she had been gripped by the thought that she would never see them again.

As they were leaving for home, with her father driving, Patricia asked, "Daddy, tell me, are you still packing heat?"

"Humm, yes. I have to. You know that!"

"Daddy, can you promise to take me to buy a gun tomorrow?"

"What? Do you mean a gun? You've always been frightened of guns. What has changed? No, never mind, I get it! Yes, we can go to the gun store if you want."

"It's not whether I want to—I must. I will not be a victim again. No, not me."

Chapter 10

Months went by with no news of another Romeo killing. In Seattle, no other reports came in of bats or flying men in strange suits. Other homicide cases were stacking up, especially during the winter when things in Seattle were gloomy and days of constant rain made for the worst depressive state.

Despite these miserable conditions in Seattle, another famous city named Portland had a new visitor named Harland to their fair city who arrived on the evening bus.

A new hunting ground with new victims, where the police have yet to discover the fatalities, thought Harland, the tall, thin stranger who waited patiently for an older adult ahead of him to disembark the bus—what he had been taught as proper etiquette. As the woman struggled with her heavy bags, he, being a gentleman, lifted the heavy carrier from the overhead bin and set it on the floor. Seeing his act of kindness, all the passengers unexpectedly applauded their approval. He turned to look at the small crowd, tilting his hat to them, then turned back as the woman struggled down the stairs.

Harland hurried past, ahead of the line, toward the gates. He reached inside his coat, removed a small flask, unscrewed the cap, and took a long drink. Ahead of him on the ramp, another bus's passengers were disembarking simultaneously, making his escape difficult. When he finally made his way clear of the bus depot, he stood briefly admiring the city with its tall skyscrapers and tall buildings.

Feeling revived, he glanced about the crowds of people. He was already eyeing some potential victims, the young girls wearing their tight, slutty clothing. So many to choose from—it boggled the senses.

Now to find shelter—protection from the rain and the police. Back in Seattle, he'd almost gotten caught. The man he'd killed—acting the fool, standing outside the apartment, hoping to get into his victim's panties. A born loser, he didn't stand a chance. The bit of hiding in the apartment shower was not to his liking. But when circumstances change, you must adapt.

That girl took some time to discover her favorite haunts. Too often, he was prepared to pounce, but her stupid ass boyfriend would show up out of the blue, ruining any chance for a righteous kill. Oh, how he dreamed of having her in his clutches, choking her to death, debasing her remains. No, it was his only pleasure in life. Nothing else could ever give him the sexual satisfaction that killing did.

She escaped and was now gone, but not before they had eyed one another. She saw his true self, the phantom of the night—death incarnate! His greatest hope was the citizens of Portland would be more generous with their tips when he performed on the streets. *Oh, not to worry, Harland. Soon you will experience what you desire most. Patience. Remember what Mommy would say: Good things come to those who wait. Oh, how I hated that woman and her whoring lovers. That damn squeaky bed.* The noise never stopped, and he was forced to sleep beneath her room as a child. *No, not until I stopped it myself.*

He recalled the sickening appearance of her in her silken bathrobe, barely covering her plump body, the smell of sex oozing from her pores. Her clients wanted coffee and breakfast the following day. Think of it, breakfast—he'd be the one starting the coffee and cooking for them, enduring their ugly smooshing until the bastards returned to their families.

But one son of a bitch didn't return to his family. The night he killed Mommy and her client—the night when it all came together.

It took some planning to end the nightmare, as he was not one to be arrested. At the time, Harland was just thirteen years old. Still, with his above-average intellect, plunging the knife into his mother's heart was more accessible than he would have guessed—but making the stupid bastard believe he did it was another problem altogether. When the man awoke and stood there coated in blood, he saw the truth—the dirty panties in his mother's mouth, her hands tied together, her corpse.

While the client prepared to run from the house, from beneath the bed, Harland—the lone avenger, complete with white face paint and a .38 revolver Mommy kept hidden in her nightstand—appeared.

Harland, pointing the gun at the defenseless man, ordered him to stop. The man began to plead for his life— the best part. Despite his cries for his life, two shots were fired into his chest—and he soon fell dead, gripping his trousers.

No, poor little man, not going home to your wife and kiddos today. No, the scoundrel was a man caught with his pants off.

That day killing his mother and her lover gave Harland such a thrill, something he could never re-create—that moment when he saw the man begging for his life and felt control over him. Although his attempts to strangle his victims—and the power he sought—gave him a temporary enthusiasm, it hadn't been anything like that day since.

He felt in charge. No, not Mommy but himself. He was free to do whatever he wanted.

After rubbing his fingerprints from the gun, he placed the murder weapon in Mommy's hands as though she was the one who fired it.

Yes, he put on an act for the coppers—the poor little boy who suffered from an alcoholic whore mother. But in the end, he was free—a no one to walk among the populous as a killer.

The cops didn't give much consideration to the type of lower-class citizen that he and his mother were in society. They'd almost believe anything, wrap up the case as a lover's argument, and file the evidence under "no one gives a shit."

In the end, how the man was shot and how his mommy was knifed in her heart were enough to convince everyone involved, and off to foster care he went.

Foster care was a joke. The first time he had a chance, he ran for the hills. He was tall for his age, and no one paid him any mind when he took up performing as a street mime, the perfect disguise. There he could walk among the crowds of people; none would guess that a true killer was near them, closer than they would ever know. He did a short stint in the circus, working the trapeze ropes and netting, and was offered a chance to join a troupe but failed because of his love for alcohol on more than one occasion—his last opportunity to fit into society.

While walking on the busy sidewalks, a sign caught his eye. In bold letters, a fortune teller advertised: *Want to know your future? Will you be successful? Come inside to see!*

Harland had just arrived and didn't want to announce his whereabouts to the police. No, if this fortune teller were worth her weight, she'd pick up on the type of man he was.

If only she were blessed with a special gift.

The room was darkened. Thick fabric curtains hung across the windows. Still, something about having his fortune told thrilled Harland, and he had to know.

A table sat in the middle of the room, covered with a white embroidered tablecloth, and in the center, as one would guess, was a crystal ball. Instantaneously, the smell of incense burning filled his nostrils—a pleasant cherry aroma.

Standing there, he wasn't sure what to do. Should he call out or stand silently like a fool? It took only a moment before an older woman greeted him, with gray streaks in her hair and a round body covered in a floral pattern dress.

"Hello, please sit at the table and make yourself comfortable. I am Madam Mikos. Tell me, traveler, what brings you to my shop? Wait, stay where you are, please."

The unexpected change in demeanor was almost scandalous to Harland. He stood frozen, gripping the chair, unsure what to do. But his crooked smile was unmistakable.

"I am discerning something about you, traveler!" she said.

"Yes, go on."

"I see blackness that covers you. I see deep pain emitting from your presence. Something that happened to you some time ago? Yes, as a child. Wait. Your mother. It began there!"

"Oh, this is good. I'm enjoying this! I thought at least you needed your spiritual convertor. Tell me, how can you read my fortune without your crystal ball?" he asked.

"No, my abilities do not depend upon parlor tricks. I see great pain and death!"

"Oh, death. Yes, go on. Please continue."

Looking at Harland, Madam Mikos nervously

shouted, "It is not my time. No, not for some time yet! But you, you will not leave this city? Here is where you will meet your end. Something, yes, something—a woman, a young female. Shots ring out, piercing your heart. The heart, your heart that hates and murders."

A broad smile appeared on Harland's face, and he responded, "Please go on. Tell me more. I'm dying to know more!"

"The woman has seen you, your true self, and escaped. She returns—that's all I know. Wait, wait, someone new to the game. Someone, the revenger, will soon be hunting you!"

"The revenger, you say? The witness returns; my heart is pierced. Pity, I have hoped for your city to provide me with suitable hunting grounds. But now it seems I've mistakenly not considered your true abilities as a fortune teller, and I find myself exposed. You spoke of these others, too, who will die at my hands. A game of cat and mouse—how thrilling. I cannot wait to play. But no matter, I can immediately remedy one problem by taking your life, much like the others who saw the true me as the life drained from their faces. You, Madam Mikos, shall be my first victim here in your lovely city of Portland!"

"Oh, that you could kill me. But I'm afraid that won't be possible." She whistled loudly, calling out the name Brutus, and a sizeable black Doberman ran into the room—barking, baring its sharp teeth.

"It seems, Madam Mikos, that today is the day you escape my clutches," Harland said. "But no matter, I'm sure we'll meet again someday."

"No, it's doubtful. I'm afraid your days are numbered. Besides, when my time comes, I will be resting comfortably in my bed, not strangled to death within your grip."

"Strangled, you say? Such a strange word. I must ask, why that word?"

"No matter, it just popped up in my head. Go while you still can, or else I say the word that would end your life!"

"Oh, what word is that?"

"The word to my dog that means to kill you by ripping your throat out! Go now before it is too late."

The dog began to advance. On its own, it already considered Harland a threat and would kill him to protect his master. With no time to waste, Harland turned and walked out a little faster than when he arrived. Slamming the door behind him, he ran out onto the sidewalk and disappeared into the crowd.

Madam Mikos, for her part, was visibly shaken. She'd never had contact with a killer before. Yes, perhaps a war veteran who struggles with depression but no one else—nothing like the experience she encountered.

Madam Mikos immediately considered calling the police and telling them an escaped killer was on the loose. Already imagining their response, she laughed—she was sure how they'd react to her, a fortune teller.

But in all fairness, she felt compelled to do something—but what? Then she remembered the girl, the young girl in the story. *Whom could she be, and where does she live?* Questions upon questions. A freebie, the man's fortune told without payment or consideration of monetary gain.

The killer set loose on the city. Damn, who could she tell? Who would believe her? Someone working for the newspapers—someone who wasn't afraid to broadcast the truth? But who? Perhaps a client, a visiting client who had befriended her.

Almost immediately, a name popped into her head—a

challenging and intelligent newspaper reporter whom she helped find her missing dog: Karen Miller.

Returning to the kitchen, she opened her phone book and searched for the names. After finding Karen's name, she grabbed her cell phone and dialed the number.

After a few rings, a familiar voice said, "Hello, this is Karen."

"Karen, thank goodness. This is Madam Mikos. I desperately need your help!"

"Madam Mikos, what's wrong?"

"Karen, can we talk? I mean in person. I'd rather not discuss what I have to say over the phone."

"Certainly. Madam Mikos, listen, I'm almost done for the day. Can we meet at a favorite haunt of mine, over on Bigamy Street and 3rd Avenue? It's called the Grasshopper Bistro."

"Yes, of course. One of the owners is a client of mine."

"Perfect. See you within the hour."

"Thank you, Karen. I mean that. I'm—"

"Save it, for now, Madam Mikos. I can already tell that something or someone has you upset. We'll get it figured out, I promise you."

"Great, see you there."

As Karen hung up, she felt troubled. Madam Mikos and her had shared some laughs in the past. Otherwise, she had some favorite recipes for Mediterranean cuisine from her but had never expected to hear the terror in her voice. She didn't want to be late for their appointment and didn't hesitate to leave the newspaper office.

After she arrived at the Grasshopper Bistro, she saw, waving from a booth, Madam Mikos and her favorite companion, Brutus, the black Doberman lying in the aisleway, next to its owner—chewing on a bone. Taking a seat at the table, Karen dropped her heavy purse beside her and sat down.

"Karen Miller, thank you for coming on such short notice!"

"Oh, believe me, Madam Mikos, I wouldn't miss this. In times past, your powers of observation have served you well. If this thing or someone has you so troubled, it must be realized as a real threat! Excuse me, but have you eaten yet? I love the coq au vin here. I promised to pick up an order for my husband when I leave here today."

"No, I'm afraid I lost my appetite. I don't feel like eating."

"I understand. Now where to begin—at the beginning, I suppose. Please tell me, what is so troubling, and how can I help?"

"Karen, I chose you because of your grit. Today in my shop I had a visitor. Almost immediately, I felt hovering darkness—or presence, if you prefer—that there stood pure exonerated evil before me. Instantly, I froze and wouldn't allow this man to come closer. I ordered him to stop as I expressed my revelations.

"The word *strangled* appeared on my lips. The man laughed, seeing the humor in the use of that particular word. A few more things were said, and he advanced. Karen, this man was out to kill me. If Brutus weren't there, I would have been murdered. I'm sure of it!"

"Okay, Madam Mikos, you realize I'm a newspaper reporter, not a cop—right?"

"Look, Karen, call me Cassia, will you please? It's my chosen name, my first name."

"Yes, of course. Cassia it is."

Cassia studied the middle-aged woman looking back, her glasses sitting just past her nose. Her hair, cut short, was partly blonde with gray streaks. Wrinkles showed her age to be over fifty, like herself. There was a roughness that spoke of nothing but the truth. An asset on her side, Karen Miller would help her in any way she could. But the real question was how to get the word out on the streets of Portland that a killer was loose and on the prowl.

"Karen, to make this as simple as I can, I need you to write an article and tell everyone in the city that a murderer is out looking for his next victim. The man is tall, over six feet, and very thin. His face looks much like a cartoon character. Sunken cheekbones, pale-looking. He smelled like alcohol; he'd been drinking recently. He wore a long coat. He had an unpleasant smell about him. Oh my god, his teeth looked like they hadn't been brushed in forever! Karen, his eyes were small, dark orbs."

"Yes, Cassia, I got it. But there is a problem. I cannot go and publish an article like that."

"Why not? It is simple enough. I told you about the killer. Now all you have to do is publish it in your newspaper. They catch this monster, and everyone goes home happy, right?"

"No, not right! For one thing, my newspaper would be sued for defamation. I would lose my job and, no doubt, my home as well. Hell, by the time the lawyers get done with me, I'd be homeless."

"Oh, I see."

"Cassia, I want to help you, truly, I do. But we cannot print something like this without sticking our noses out. There has to be another way."

"I do not care about another way. Karen, please believe me. I saw this man bare-faced. I looked into his eyes. I heard his voice, speaking of death. There was something else—the girl, the young girl."

A waitress appeared with a smile plastered on her face. "Hello and welcome to Grasshoppers. What can I get you to drink?"

"Wine, I'll take a glass of wine," Cassia announced.

"What the heck, me, too. A glass of Pino Noir. Hey, listen, I haven't eaten all day. Could you give me your coq au vin, an order to go for my husband, when I leave today?"

"Yes, certainly."

Turning to Cassia, the waitress asked, "Madam Mikos, would you like to order something?"

"Yes, the onion soup, please."

"Great, I will be back with your wine. Thank you."

Alone together again, Karen sat back and stared at her friend.

"I'm sorry, truly I am, but do not give up. I'm pretty savvy when I want to be. Besides, I know some people. One that comes to mind is a cop—the most ruthless and callous man I know: Sergeant Berkshire, who's a mean son of a gun! Besides him, I have some contacts out on the street. When this stranger appears, people will first want to know who he is. Next, they'll ask, 'Is the man Trouble with a capital T?' Street people, much like inmates inside a prison, feel the city's heartbeat. This invader won't get too far without being noticed. When he does, we'll hear about it. Relax, Cassia. I'm sure everything will turn out fine."

"I'm still troubled by the woman I saw in my vision. Whom could she be? She kills someone, a crusader of sorts. I saw her firing the gun."

Silence for a short time. Then Karen smiled and said, "For now, I wouldn't consider going out at night by yourself—no, not without your friend Brutus. Besides, there's truth in that old saying: A dog is man's best friend. No, the reality is dogs are also a woman's best friend and protector. I imagine that today Brutus saved your life!"

"I announced to that monster that today wasn't my time to die—I'm to die in my bed."

Instantaneously, Cassia's expression changed, and she

looked at Karen; all color faded from her face.

"Karen, tell me, and please be honest: You don't suppose he's my killer, do you? This man is the one that murders me in my bed?"

Silence. Karen stared back at Madam Mikos with no words.

Chapter 11

Harland considered Portland his new home. On such a day as this—the sunshine overhead, the slight breeze filling his nostrils, with the smell of flowers blooming near the busy city sidewalks. Although he had only been here a short time, bumming change from the residents seemed easier. His little act of the funny mime making silly gestures on the sidewalks worked out nicely.

Portland was not the penny-pincher crowd of Seattle. Portland proper and its citizens were free to give away some pocket change for his little act. Besides all this, what mattered most was his ability to hide in plain sight. This truth allowed him to be particular about his next victim— and, as if on cue, she was just a few feet away from arriving for work.

Harland currently lives in a tent in the Old Town neighborhood with many other homeless, the central location for many crucial social services in the city. He blended in perfectly among them.

He eyed the young brunette hurrying down the sidewalk to reach her building, not taking the time to look his way. None of the residents gave the homeless population any mind.

Today he decided to drop off the note—*the* note— which would give him such a thrill. The one Harland wrote for her alone. He wouldn't miss her reaction. To see the little slut reading it, where it described her doom, somehow made him feel alive with enthusiasm.

Nearby on the busy street where she parked her car was the place he decided to begin his performance that morning. The truth is that no one was into mimes in the morning; his best chance for any money always came at night when the good citizens were tanked up with alcohol so they could easily be made the fool. Still, an opportunity to drop off his little note onto her windshield wouldn't be missed.

Dancing and hopping as a musical melody played in his head, Harland smiled at those he met and tipped his hat. Not far down the busy street, the dented yellow Toyota was parked.

Inching closer, he paused briefly, and when no one was watching, he took his note, pulled back the windshield wipers, and was about to allow them to snap back in place when a noise came down the street—loud music playing drums and horned instruments.

He froze, withdrawing backward. He removed the tiny card and placed it back inside his pocket. He recognized the tune to mean one thing: The circus was in town.

As he and everyone watched, a bright-colored pink Cadillac appeared, blowing its horns with clowns behind the wheel—not the usual Portland drivers but actual clowns. Behind them was a long procession of vehicles hauling a small assortment of animals. The circus was undoubtedly already at the fairgrounds, but everyone loves a clown unless you perform as one. There, in front of the Cadillac, were two motorcycle cops, distracted by the sounds and loud noises.

Harland walked back to the sidewalk and slipped into the crowd of spectators, away from the approaching cops. Slowly, the caravan crawled along the roadway, the crowds gathered, and the circus performers went into their routine of enticing the masses to join them at the big top.

As a group of clowns followed the trailers, walking alongside, Hartland unexpectedly recognized one clown: McBride, the crossdresser, wearing his dress and rainbow-colored wig, overly large breasts, a red nose, and bright red painted lips. The silly shoes, as always, carried a large flower bouquet with his signature trademark—a small flying bee—circling atop the flowers in a make-believe attempt to make it seem real. Children seemed mesmerized when the bee suddenly grew three times its size and landed on their heads. Then, swiping at the bee, McBride captured it in his hand and made it disappear to the wonder of children and adults alike.

Surprise. Above all wonder, the girl that was to be Harland's next conquest appeared in public, near her office on the sidewalk.

Oh, I see you there. Coming out to see the circus, are you? Harland thought. He saw her there among the crowds of spectators, all dressed up, much like a slut in heat!

A chill ran down his back. *The thrill of having her within my clutches, the little tramp. Look at the men checking out her body, their lost hopes of conquest. No worries, you desperate fools. Soon this little temptation will be gone from your sight!* His chosen victim was not far away, only six feet or so.

Still hidden, Harland waited until McBride finished his little routine and continued on his way. When the spectacle moved down the street, Harland immediately went into his act, performing as a street mime. Gratefully, he believed all around him would consider him part of the circus, the lone performer who again made fun of the unsuspecting populace.

Harland moved down the street, closer to his intended victim, but something happened that caused him an unexpected panic from within his spirit.

The crowds slowly dispersed around him. Suddenly, standing by herself, the young beauty was looking directly at him, watching his every move. Sheer panic shocked him. He was always hidden in his private world. None was allowed to see his true self. Only briefly, he froze.

Mere seconds later, he went into his skit and approached her. His white painted face and the black derby hat made the illusion genuine—no words, only the waving of his hands, hidden beneath his gloves.

Unexpectedly, a group of spectators had gathered to watch. But it didn't matter! No, caught in his spider web, this innocent little moth could do nothing to escape. He was dancing around her. He stopped and stared straight ahead. Frozen in place, he waited for her reaction. The outburst of laughter intrigued him. This little harlot seemingly wasn't afraid. She bravely looked at him. She was not merely staring at him but through his soul—which somehow felt unnerving.

Playfully, he danced around her and removed a flower from his lapel. Handing it to her, he smiled and bowed politely. Just as she took the flower from his hand, it deflated.

Hearing oohs and ahhs from the crowd, Harland danced around her again. She bowed, being polite. This time, however, he placed the flower close to his heart. Magically, it doubled in size as he handed it to her again.

Clapping erupted from the crowd, and he continued his dance, away from the people as far away as he could, and ducked into a back alley, panting.

He returned to his cardboard hut a block away, jumped inside, and searched for the remaining bottle of vodka. He unscrewed the cap and downed a couple of long swigs, the whole while asking himself, *what happened back on the street? Who in the hell does this girl think she is to outperform me?*

It all began to make sense, more apparent than before. The bitch was obviously supposed to refuse the flower—then next, for all to see, he'd be sad, the damn flower would deflate again, and he would walk away, supposedly heartbroken. Damn it, that was how it's supposed to go—not bow in return and take the flower from his hand! *No, no, this will never work! Who in the hell does she think she is to upstage me?*

Harland, downing another drink, thought, *not only will she be my next victim, but she will die slowly for her insolence!* Another harsh reality struck him as he realized he left so quickly that he never got any money for his act. *Damn that bitch for ruining everything! She is going to die. Yes, she will die and bleed. But is it enough to simply die? No, she needs to suffer!*

Next, he heard tiny steps outside his cardboard shelter. Just outside, unexpectedly, Harland heard voices talking.

A female voice said, "Hello, I enjoyed your performance. Can I speak to you for a moment?"

Chapter 12

Shortly after roll call, Stevens moseyed to his desk. After being joined by his partner, Matthews, they sat down across from one another.

"What can I do? Monica wants to get a divorce."

"Not much, old buddy. Do you now see the reason for me staying single?" Stevens said.

"Yeah, but ever since we lost our daughter, things between her and I haven't been the same."

"As I said, I'm no expert on marital affairs. But from what I understand, when tragedy strikes, if the marriage had cracks in it from before that were never realized, then it cannot stand the pressure and breaks. Whereas true love, the genuine kind, finds its way back from ruin and is stronger than before. Will this happen to your marriage? Who knows? Maybe the lonely nights waiting for that phone call have become too much for Lisa, and she can't do it any longer. As I said, though, I'm not an expert."

"Yeah, you're not an expert!"

As luck would have it, a man appeared at Stevens's desk. Standing over six feet with broad shoulders, he wore a black beard with an array of tattoos down his forearms—the usual biker type.

"Excuse me, are you Stevens, the homicide detective?"

"Yes, I'm Stevens. How can I help you?"

"I'm Jack, Jack McIntyre. I'm also Andy McIntyre's

brother, the guy you found in the trash dumpster a couple of months ago."

"Oh yes, hello. I'm sorry for your loss."

"Thank you for your sentiment, but what I want to know is what happened to my brother. What have you found out about the killer? I have to say I can't believe anyone could overpower Andy. He was the best fighter I knew. He kicked my ass once or twice."

"Look, this isn't exactly the place. Why don't you follow me? We have a room, and we can speak more quietly without the phone ringing constantly in our ears."

"Yeah, why not?"

The pair left behind Matthews to ponder his future of not being married.

Stevens led Jack to a back room and closed the door behind him. Pausing only briefly, he chose his words carefully. "Would you care for a coffee or something?"

"Sure, if you have some brewing."

"No problem. I'll be right back. How do you like it—cream or sugar?"

"No, straight up—the darker, the better. Black tar if you have it."

"Got it. Be right back."

Returning a short time later with the two coffees in hand, Stevens handed one to Jack and sat down, apologizing for what happened to Andy.

"Look, Jack, again, I am sorry about your brother."

"Tell me, how did he die?"

"Your brother was strangled to death. From what we could ascertain, the killer used a wire of some type."

"A wire?"

"Yes, but that's not all. From what we could figure, your brother was tracking the man we named the Romeo killer, a serial killer here in our city who pursued young women, usually living in high-rise complexes."

"Andy? That doesn't sound right! He assuredly would have confronted the guy and strangled him to death, not the other way around!"

"Look, I believe your brother was acting as the hero in this case and was trying to warn these women that someone was tracking them and hunting them, much like a lion would pursue prey."

"Andy? Look, he had the toughest time fitting into society after becoming disfigured by losing his arm and the burns on his face in the war. That's the reason he turned to alcohol, I suppose. But to me, it still doesn't make any sense."

"Redemption, I suppose. Maybe Andy thought if he could tell these women about this guy, he could save their lives. Sadly, the notes on their cars weren't enough. Besides, no one would believe a note! Hell, it could be from anyone!"

"A note, you say? What type of note?"

"Well, a sort of poem if you wish. Did you know that your brother loved Shakespeare? He would often end the note in a scene from a Shakespearian play. Alas, no one paid him any mind."

"Andy. That would make sense. He appreciated the arts and tried out for a part in a play in high school but lost out to a better-looking guy, I'm afraid."

"There is something else. I caught a glimpse of the killer."

"Tell me, did you shoot the son of a bitch?"

"No, but this guy leaped off a seventh-floor balcony."

"So, he doesn't fear heights, I take it?"

"No, not this guy. He leaped out over the balcony wearing a black outfit with a parachute. He was long gone when we made it to the ground floor to give chase."

"What was he doing there anyway? What brought this guy to that particular apartment complex?"

"Simply stated, his next victim!"

"What do you mean, his next victim?"

"I still can't divulge too many details in the case—it's still an ongoing investigation—but this young woman had found a note, much like the others. Lucky for her, the killer chose someone else to be his next victim. Otherwise, she, too, would have been strangled."

"So where is she now? Is there a way I could talk to her?"

"No, I'm afraid not. This particular witness has flown the coop, so to speak."

"Yeah, okay, but wasn't she a witness or something?"

"No, not really. How can I say this? Thinking back at the time when we found your brother's body in the dumpster, this witness came forward—not a witness but someone with a shred of evidence. She found a note, apparently written by your brother, that warned her she was being watched. I'd never seen anything like this before when she realized this warning could be meant for her. I mean that when she found the note under her broken-down car, she had had enough and wasn't taking any chances. She called her father and told her parents she was coming home! Assuming all was safe, I suggested she get her belongings and meet me at my car. How was I to know the killer was still in her apartment waiting for her, waiting to strangle her?"

"Oh man, this guy had it bad, it sounds like!"

"Oh, let me tell you. You don't know half of it. When my witness caught a glimpse of something in her shower, she screamed and ran for the hills. Sadly, the guy she was talking to at the time didn't get it. But he soon understood when this strangler took a kitchen knife and jabbed it in his eye!"

Jack removed his coat and placed it at the back of his chair. "Damn, no fooling!"

Stevens instantly noticed the tattoo displaying the anchor, the eagle, and the trident on Jack's forearm, representing the Navy Seals.

"So, tell me, where have you served?" Stevens asked.

"Mainly overseas is about all I can tell you. It's the reason I wasn't here sooner to receive my brother's remains. Look, you have a mom—right? Well, I not only have a mother but four sisters as well. I received a phone call, an alarming phone call from my mother crying her eyes out! She explained that Andy was found dead in a trash dumpster. Can you fucking imagine my brother, a war hero, thrown away like garbage! No, I'm afraid, Detective Stevens, this will never do."

"I completely understand your family's disappointment. But tell me, Jack, what is it you plan to do? Look, we cannot have any vigilantes running through our city streets looking to take justice on their own and kill anyone they suspect, you understand?"

"I understand you have an ongoing investigation, but could you tell me how long it has been since your last murder or strangulation? Or has anyone received a note describing their deaths like before?"

"All right, step back for a minute. Here, Jack! As I said, I feel for you and your family, but I'm not handing you the keys to our city so you can go on the prowl and seek out this guy. It's not done that way, and you know this. I shouldn't have to say anything, but here I go: If I catch you harassing anyone, I'll run your ass in for something— I don't know what. But I'll figure out something, believe you me!"

"Calm down, Stevens. Look, we're both on the same

side here. Something you have no way of knowing is that I have done some investigations a time or two for the department of the Navy Judge Advocate General's office. Now all I'm asking for is a little cooperation. Could you tell me where my brother lived or his favorite haunts—you know, the places he most enjoyed visiting?"

"Jack, all right. Here's something you must understand. Your brother was homeless and lived on the streets. He lived the life of an alcoholic. He was reduced to begging for change and digging for food in trash cans. I'm afraid he didn't live the life of a war hero. But there was someplace—yes, a favorite place—that treated him with respect, you could say, a little dive named the Tin Cup. A girl was working there named Penny who took a liking to your brother. She knew more about him than anyone else. I would start there. But nowadays, with Covid and all and people losing their jobs, who knows if she still works there?"

"It's a start. Look, if I come across my brother's killer, I promise I won't kill the guy unless he tries to kill me, all right?"

"Fine, I'd start there. You should know something: There hasn't been strangulation matching the Romeo murders here in Seattle for several months. It seems our killer has been arrested or he's dead. The latter would be fine with me."

"True, but if our paths cross—this killer and me—I can only say I pity the fool. Afterward, you can get what's left."

"Fair enough. Look, I have to run, police work and all. Oh, before I go, there is the matter of your brother's personal belongings. Apart from the dirty blankets and cardboard he used for shelter, there was a small cigar box filled with sketching pens and paper. You know, the items he used to create the warning cards."

"Oh, I see."

"Come follow me. I have something to give you."

The pair descended some stairs to the basement and continued to an iron gate partition—the overhead sign read: POLICE IMPOUND. Stevens informed a guard inside he was there to pick up something and after signing his name on a clipboard, he asked for evidence box number 439567.

After a short time, the guard returned, slid the box through the opening, and returned to work inside.

At a table nearby, Stevens pulled open the lid and looked inside. He pushed aside the prosthetic arm and smelly coat.

"Here it is," Stevens announced, then removed a small cigar box wrapped in plastic. Much like everything else, he pulled it free and stared at it briefly.

Next, handing it to Jack, he said, "Here. I want you to have this. Perhaps you will want to give it to your mother for sentimental reasons or to remember your brother."

"What is it?"

"It's the cigar box in which your brother Andy kept his drawings and sketching equipment. We found it next to the trash bin."

Jack said thank you and reached for his backpack. Unzipping it, he slipped it inside, closed the flap, and hoisted it across his shoulders.

"Detective Stevens, you have your phone with you, right?"

"Yes, strapped to my hip. Why?"

"Call this number. It's my home number, in case you want to reach me for something."

"Okay, shoot. Got it. Look, I'll send you a text in a little while. Look for a 206 area code."

"Detective Stevens, thank you for your help. My family and I appreciate it. Tell me, where is this Tin Cup located?"

"About three miles from here on the boulevard. Head west, and you can't miss it! Although I must warn you, parking is a bitch."

"No worries. I prefer walking. I need to get my feeling back in my legs after such a long flight."

"What? How long ago did you arrive back in the US?"

"About eight hours ago. I caught a ride-along from New York. Along the way, I slept when I could. If nothing else, you'll soon discover I'm relentless!"

"Yes, all right. If you require anything, please let me know. And watch your back out there. Seattle city streets can be dangerous."

Finding the detective's statement humorous, Jack replied, "No, you're wrong. In Afghanistan, the city streets are what's dangerous. Having someone's throat slit for a few pennies is the norm. That's how they settle arguments there. I must be going, Stevens. Again, thanks for the coffee."

"Sure thing! Listen, something that wasn't mentioned earlier: The man we believe to be the Romeo Strangler seems to be an opportunist assassin. I mean that a body was found in the apartment of a woman named Patricia Harper. Although we believe the strangler was there to murder her, something happened that made him change his plans."

"So, what you're saying is this guy doesn't particularly fit the mold of a serial strangler?"

"Yes. That's exactly what I'm saying."

"Look, Stevens, a murderer is a murderer—no matter the title you give them. I've killed in the line of duty. At night I can see the faces of the ones I've killed."

"You're not alone in being haunted by the lives you've snuffed out. We call it in the line of duty. But no matter the title you place on it, I have to sleep at night. Most times, it's difficult. Besides this, I wanted to thank you for your service."

"Hum, yeah, I suppose. But thanking me for doing my job is a bit over the top. I get it that a grateful nation has to show its appreciation somehow. I wish they showed my brother more respect for his sacrifice."

"True enough. Seattle is a small enough city. I'm sure we'll run into each other again."

"I hope so, Detective."

"Now, if you will excuse me, I have police work. Come on. I'll show you out."

Jack followed Stevens to the front lobby, shook his hand, and walked onto the rainy Seattle streets. The rain was steady but not a downpour—more or less a nuisance. Pulling his hood over his head, he lifted his backpack across his shoulders and headed west. Although it was twenty minutes before five in the afternoon, the evening traffic rush hadn't started. Still, the sidewalks seemed crowded with pedestrians.

Taking his time to survey his surroundings, Jack considered these streets where his brother Andy had lived. Although a naval hospital was not far, when Andy was discharged, he remained living here in this busy urban environment. Perhaps he intended that Jackie would change her mind and take him back. Maybe he hoped she would look past his disfigurement and still want to be married. Who knows what he was thinking? But Jack realized the constant dreary rain indeed couldn't help his depressive state of mind.

Determined, Jack continued on his trek. Occasionally, someone would bump into him, and he was unsure if they mistakenly took him as a tourist and tried to pickpocket his wallet. Either way, catching a hand brush up against his person was met with an opposing grip and callous stare, which startled the would-be assailant.

Notwithstanding, he soon saw ahead the flashing small neon sign: THE TIN CUP. He walked through the door and instantly heard a favorite rock 'n' roll tune. Jack shook off the raindrops from his coat and looked around.

The evening rush of patrons had yet to arrive. The bar, lined with several vacant chairs, was primarily available to anyone choosing a seat. The rest of the restaurant tables were also scarcely filled with customers. Seeing the sign: PLEASE SEAT YOURSELF, Jack looked for a suitable place he could gather his thoughts.

There, not far away, the outside patio was utterly empty. Jack found an open table near a kerosene heater. He removed his all-weather jacket and backpack, then sat down.

There at each table were menus tucked between the napkin holders. Grabbing one, he quickly surveyed the contents. Not a five-course meal or anything like that, but the American favorite cheeseburger and fries were still a sure fix for his hunger pains.

After a while, a waitress appeared, apologizing for being late. Her name, as fate would have it, was Penelope. At first glance, she looked to be in her early twenties with the usual height and build, along with a little round bottom. Her brown hair was tied up in a bun behind her head.

"Hello, welcome to the Tin Cup. Would you like to hear our specials?"

"No, thank you. All I want is a cheeseburger and fries."

"Okay, great. Would you care for a drink?"

"Yes, tell me what's on tap."

"Oh, this week, I believe we have Samuel Adams."

"Great, I'll take one of those!"

"All right, I'll be right back with your order."

"Oh, Penelope, before you go, can I ask you a question?"

"Yes, certainly. Ask me anything. But please call me Penny; it's what all my friends call me."

"Penny, do you remember a veteran named Andy, a guy who lost one arm and part of his face was burned? He used to frequent this establishment."

"Andy? Yes. I helped him out a time or two when I could, you understand. He was homeless, and I felt sorry for him. Besides that, Andy was a nice man who treated all the servers here respectfully, ensuring we got to our cars safely. Why? Did you know Andy?"

"Yes, you could say that. Andy was my brother. My name is Jack McIntyre. Glad to meet you."

"Oh?"

"I'm here to discover who killed my brother."

"Oh, I see. Let me get your order. Before we get too busy, I'll return, and we can talk about dear, sweet Andy."

"That's great. Thank you, Penelope—I mean Penny."

"Hey, no problem. As I said, Andy was a great person. I was sad to hear he died."

"Me, too. But no, he didn't die in his bed or anything like that—he was murdered, and I intend on finding out who did it!"

"As I said, I will help you in any way I can. I'll be right back."

Penny returned with a tall beer in her hand. After setting it down she hurried over to a group of customers that unexpectedly appeared—a large party of eight. Taking their orders, she again disappeared and returned to them with a tray full of drinks. While the party waited for their food order, she promptly sat at Jack's table and stared out the window at the sidewalks just beyond.

"This was Andy's favorite place to sit. I find it strange

that you chose this table."

"My brother sat here, did he now? Please tell me, did Andy have friends or anything like that?"

"No, I wouldn't say friends. But being homeless here in Seattle, there is a whole community of homeless people that have gathered to survive, living here on these rainy streets—mainly because of the drug use. That's a problem here in the city."

"Did Andy ever talk about seeing some stalker or menacing figure carousing the streets? Did he ever confide in you or tell you to beware of the boogie man?"

"No, nothing like that!"

Catching a glimpse of some customers sitting at an available table on the patio, Penny excused herself and said, "I'll be right back."

"Okay, Penny, I'm not in any hurry to leave. Besides, I only arrived back in the US about nine hours ago. I'm not going anywhere."

Leaning back in his chair, he sipped his beer and stared out the window. There ahead of him, he saw the busy Seattle sidewalks were suddenly filled, becoming a crowded thoroughfare. *What did Andy see that was not obvious to the world around him? What was so special or unique that caused him to reach out to some unsuspecting woman and warn her that she was being watched?* Jack's mind raced as the unknown and mysterious became clouded with more questions than answers.

The pedestrians streamed by on the sidewalk, but Jack knew that all was not as it seemed; the whole story of the city's inhabitants was mainly hidden from view. Yes, dressed appropriately, the crowds of people busied themselves with one thing in mind: to get where they were going as quickly as possible. It would be most bothersome to discover a disruption in the schedule by receiving a note on their windshield.

Still, there it was—Andy's warning to the women. But why didn't Andy go to the police? Did hate blind him from crossing paths with the men and women in blue who might cause him such aversion that he couldn't bring himself to do it? What happened to the war hero he knew growing up?

This man alone was responsible for saving the lives of three of his fellow soldiers. There were no straightforward answers to be had.

Penny, sitting down to catch her breath, uttered, "Boy, talk about getting busy all of a sudden! Jack, how's your beer?"

"Truthfully, almost gone."

"Would you like another?"

"Yeah—you bet. But after you have caught your breath. Like I said, no hurry."

"I'll be right back."

"No, wait a minute. Penny, before you go, is there anything else you can tell me about Andy?"

"Well, let's see. Andy liked to draw. I know that much—there is a detective named Stevens; he was the guy who found your brother's remains. He told me they found plastic bags containing your brother's personal belongings at the crime scene."

"I have the cigar box with me—nothing much to speak of, only a few sketches. I have it here in my backpack. I haven't dared to open it. Anything else?"

"Well, there were some homeless guy's Andy would occasionally share a drink. One of them is named Patrick, and the other is Harper. Your brother would sometimes hang with them when they gave blood to get a few bucks so that they could buy themselves a bottle. But mostly, Andy avoided them if he could. What I mean is the guy called Harper argued your brother's injuries were from a car crash, not sustained in the war overseas."

"Oh! So, Penny, tell me, where can I find these so-called friends of Andy's?"

"From what I've been told, they have a homeless community under the freeway overpass. It's lined with all manner of cardboard houses. You can't miss it."

"Great."

"No worries. Look, your order is up. I'll be right back."

Now alone, Jack thought it was time to look at his brother's artwork. Unzipping his backpack and removing the cigar box, he tore open the plastic bag labeled EVIDENCE. When he opened the lid, he saw a few dollars, pencils, and paper.

One picture stood out among the rest. Surprisingly, it was the exact depiction of the Seattle sidewalk across the street. There in the picture were groups of people walking. The details were refined and exacting: the storefronts with their displays in the windows, the buildings' stucco and graphics, the women and men under various colored umbrellas, and the rain coming down.

Jack stared intensely at the details. There to the trained eye—hard to see, easily overlooked—was a face in the shadows. Jack held the picture up to the light. Yes, some person was drawn in faded gray and white. The shape of what appeared to be a round head and white face stared directly at the artist—his brother.

Unexpectedly, Penny appeared with the cheeseburger and fries. "Here you go! I hope you enjoy it."

"Penny, you wouldn't happen to have a magnifying glass, would you?"

"What? No."

"I need to enlarge this drawing somehow."

"Well, Janey, our manager, has a computer and fax

machine. We could scan the picture to the computer and magnify the image that way."

"You're a genius, Penny. Do you have time to do it now?"

"No, sir. Not now. The customers are stacking up. The customers usually slow down around ten o'clock, and we're not as busy. We could do it then if you want. What did you see in the picture?" Penny asked.

"I'm not sure—a face perhaps. Nothing more."

"Hurry and eat your cheeseburger before it's cold. I'll be back to check on you. How's your beer? Still, need another?"

"Yes, absolutely."

"Waitress, could you bring me some ketchup when you have time?" a woman called out from another table.

Penny apologized to her customers and said, "Yes, I'll be there in a minute."

After she ran off to attend to her customers, Jack had no more begun to cut his burger in two when a woman whispered at the table next to him.

"Excuse me. I couldn't help but overhear you asking for a magnifying glass."

Jack turned to see an older woman and her husband glancing over their menus. "Yes, do you have one handy?"

"Oh, my husband Delbert can't see worth a darn. I always bring one with us every time we go out to eat."

"I'll take the fish and chips," Delbert announced, then reached out and handed Jack the magnifying glass.

"Thank you, sir. I promise I won't be but a minute."

"Take your time, son. I already told Betty what I want to order."

Now with the magnifying glass, details in his brother's sketch came alive. Jack could see the image of someone. Yes, someone was standing, barely visible but probably oblivious to those walking past.

Jack took the card and flipped it over. On the back was an inscription that read: *The Jackal is watching!*

Now the certainty of what he was looking at struck him as Jack realized this fiend was dressed as a mime, complete with a derby hat.

Chapter 13

Later that day, Karen Miller planned on meeting police Sergeant Berkshire for coffee. She had just finished drafting a public notice and stared at her results. She hoped to post a bulletin about how people need to beware of unknown strangers—including don't go out at night alone.

No, that wouldn't do. Aside from sounding foolish, it would be useless to anyone. Being a creative newspaper gal, if Karen had direction, she was sure she could put the words together on paper. But she needed to figure out how best to communicate this message. Good thing she knew a police sergeant to give her suggestions. Still not satisfied, *perhaps more polish is in order*, she thought.

It had been weeks since she had last met Madam Mikos. Bothered with the realization that she could meet her end by being strangled to death, she had booked a flight that evening and returned to Greece for a visit. She wasn't exactly sure when she was returning home.

Although there had been reports of strange deaths in the city, nothing like mutilations or beheadings caught everyone's attention. Besides the usual drug activity, burglary and rape seemed calm in the city.

Still, she couldn't get over Cassia's quick departure.

Over the years, both she and Madam Mikos had become friends. To Karen, the occasional tea readings and future predictions were silly at best. Although she could predict the location of Karen's lost cat, everything else, for the most part, seemed hard to believe— especially about her gaining notoriety as a newspaper reporter and receiving a Pulitzer Prize for journalism.

Still, Cassia was a hoot and fun to be around, especially when she had too much wine. But if there was something to this stranger, she encountered in her shop, who was to say? Looking at the time, Karen realized she had to run. So, after locking up her desk, she reached down, grabbed her heavy purse, and left her office. She placed an X in the out column on the office board near the door and hurried out.

While unlocking her car Karen's phone rang unexpectedly. Reaching into the hallows of the large compartment, she grabbed her phone and said, "Hello, this is Karen."

"Mrs. Miller, this is Sergeant Berkshire. I'm afraid I will have to cancel our meeting this morning. Something has come up at the station. Could we make it another time?"

"Yes, certainly. But I must tell you this is the second time you've canceled our meeting, Sergeant Berkshire. Truthfully, I'm beginning to get a complex."

Laughing on the phone, the sergeant said, "Karen, you floor me, I swear. No, please listen. I had every intention of keeping our get-together. But this morning at roll call, I was informed that the vice president is coming to town next week for a democratic convention, so all hands on deck. Sure, maybe if it was the president himself. But a vice president, why the fuss?"

It was Karen's turn to laugh. She gladly agreed to meet another time and hung up. She got into her car, ready to leave. She pondered on whether to return to work. After craving some chocolate eclairs, she started her car and drove off.

On the way, she drove passed Madam Miko's place of business. Surprised to see the lights on, she turned at the next block, followed it to the next street, returned, and parked in front of the building.

After getting out of her car, she approached the door and looked inside. There, to her amazement, she saw Cassia vacuuming her carpets. She briefly caught Cassia's attention. Cassia looked troubled as she ushered Karen to come inside.

When Cassia shut off the vacuum, Karen asked, "Cassia, when did you get home? Why didn't you call me? I could have picked you up from the airport."

"There has been a development. Something has changed!"

"What do you mean by something has changed?"

"The man I saw—the man who threatened me."

"What about him? Look, I'm glad to see you home! Speaking of that man you saw, I've been trying to meet with Sergeant Berkshire to review some ideas on making posters. But the guy is so busy that he keeps canceling on me!"

"No, Karen, you do not understand. The cravings to strangle and murder have been diminished. I'm afraid to say, the killer..." She trailed off.

"What about the killer, Madam Mikos?"

Turning to Karen with a star-gazed expression, she whispered, "The killer is in love."

"What? How in the world would you know such a thing?"

"Come in. Hurry. Sit down at the table, and I'll show you what I mean."

"How are you going to do that? Oh wait, I get it—my fortune. You're going to tell me my fortune, right?"

"No, nothing like that! Besides, it's not about you,

Karen. It's about the man—the man who's a serial killer."

"All right, what now? What I mean is, how can, you be sure?"

"To the ever-nonbeliever doubters such as yourself, I say phooey!"

"Oh, Cassia, I didn't mean to upset you—we've been friends for many years. Now listen to me for a moment. I can see that you're really into this fortune-telling stuff. So, I have a suggestion: Why not show me how you can tell the future? What do you say? Better yet, tell me where we can find this serial killer, and I'll tell my police friend Sergeant Berkshire."

"Look, Karen, it will not work if you're a doubter. You seem the biggest doubter of them all if you don't mind me saying!"

"No insult taken. So why not show me how you do it?"

"All right. But before I can, we must clear the room of any negative energy."

"How do we do that?"

"Karen, do you remember the first time you came to me looking for your cat?"

"Yes, of course. I was somewhat frightened at the time, thinking about how Tommy was run over by a truck or something."

"Yes, that same concentration must be produced now. Give me a moment, let me put away my vacuum, and I'll be right back."

"All right. But before you go, I have a question: Why can't you simply track the man's whereabouts telepathically?"

"Simple. I don't have that power of observation. That would take a true psychic."

"Is there such a person—living, I mean?"

"I have personally known of only one such man."

"Well, there you have it. Call your psychic friend, and ask him to tell you where the serial killer is hiding. Seems simple enough to me, right?"

"No, I'm afraid I cannot reach him, ye of little faith in my abilities." Cassia began laughing. "Besides, I already did," she admitted, "but was unsuccessful."

"That's too bad. Okay, back to helping the doubter—me—what do you want me to do?"

"Wait here. I'll be right back, all right?"

"Sure, I'll sit here patiently until you return."

"Fine. I'll only be a moment, I promise you."

Five minutes later, Cassia returned, dressed in dark silk clothing.

"All right, Karen, listen to me, please. I need you to clear your mind of all outside influences."

"I'm not certain I can do that."

"Yes, yes, of course. Listen, I have an idea I use when confronted with difficult clients. Try this: Look straight ahead at the crystal ball in the center of the table, stare deeply into it, and listen to my voice. My voice is only a path to follow. Where you go is entirely up to you. But in all of this, I want you to relax. Can you do that, Karen—relax, I mean?"

"Yes, I believe so."

"Excellent. Let us begin. I want you to travel to your favorite vacation destination."

"Yes, got it!"

"Next, imagine yourself with your husband. The two of you have just finished a delicious meal. From your vantage point, you can see the moon at its lowest point in the sky. So romantic, so relaxing."

"Yes, that would be Bonaire, on our twenty-fifth anniversary."

"Now focus on nothing else about that night."

"Yes, it was amazing."

"Now, with the memory fresh in your mind and your thoughts distracted from the stress of your job, watch me as I begin to shuffle the Tarot cards before us. However, my concentration will be solely on the man I saw in my shop. Now let us begin."

As Karen watched, Cassia began shuffling the large cards, laying the cards down—the first card, Knight of Wands, the second, Queen of Cups, and so forth. But when cards from the Major Arcana began to appear and were laid down, they consisted mainly of three unique cards: The Lovers, The Devil, and Death.

Madam Mikos sat back, sighed, and said, "There is your proof. What else can I say?"

"Oh, I see, or do I?"

"Yes, Karen, there is proof before your eyes. What's not to understand?"

"To me, the novice, I don't understand. What do you see? I need an interpreter."

"You're an intelligent woman by all accounts. Yet, you cannot see."

"By all means, break it down for me, Madam Mikos."

"All in all, the cards that matter most are these three: The Devil, meaning the man is influenced by evil intent. Next, The Lovers—the most surprising to me—how is it possible? Death is always a crowd favorite; I'm being facetious. Still, there you have it!"

"Yes, there it is, I suppose. It would be nice to have your psychic friend around to tell us where this killer is living."

"Certainly, you're right. It would be nice, wouldn't it? Karen, did you happen to notice the Eight of Swords tarot card?"

"Yes, I see it. What's unique about that card?"

"Simple. It comes as a warning that your thoughts and beliefs are no longer serving you."

"Whose thoughts are you talking about—yours or the killers?"

"Yes, plainly the killer—I have concentrated on the killer and no one else except for a split second. My thoughts drifted."

"Drifted, how?"

"A memory of my daughter, away at college. But I have a thought about my daughter that's unclear. Deception is being played out."

Amid silence and blank stares, the two women gazed at one another, seeking answers.

"Cassia, there was something else that I failed to mention. Earlier, when I was distracted by the memory of Bonaire, I saw a number flash before my eyes—not my eyes but perhaps my third eye. It's believed to be linked to perception."

"Oh, tell me."

"The number 925," Karen announced.

"Isn't that number a material element for silver? Sterling silver, to be exact? In the past, some stories involved that number or the 925 angel number. Your guardian angel thinks of you. Your angel is aware of your state of mind and calling out loud for a change in your situation. But this is not possible if you keep crossing your arms. You would have to seek the transformation you desire in your life. Rejoice since the number 925 indicates a radical metamorphosis or a stage of transit."

"All right, tell me, does the number or the name Sterling mean anything?" Karen asked.

"Yes! It certainly does. Sterling is the name of the psychic I told you about."

"Oh, I see. My perception tells me strange events are

about to unfold. But I don't know why I said this."

"Yes, forces are at work. But what type are they? Do you suppose I should answer the phone?"

"The phone? I don't hear—"

The phone rang in the next room. Cassia and Karen looked at one another, unsure what to do.

Chapter 14

Jack McIntyre continued to stare at the details of the drawing. Was there something else hidden there in the lead lines? Something no one took the time to examine?

His cell phone rang. After looking at the caller's ID, he refused to answer it and slipped it back into his pants pocket.

"Aren't you going to answer it?" Penny appeared, asking the question.

"No, not now. I mean, maybe later. Why are you concerned?"

"Oh, please forgive me. I thought that perhaps it was your wife checking on you or some other nonsense!"

"Wife, me?"

"Forget it. I'm just acting silly."

"No, it's fine. Look, Penny, I'm only here for a short time. My brother was killed, and I intend on finding the bastard who did it."

"Jack, isn't that for the police to discover?"

"Yes, I'm sure you're right. Hey, let's forget all that stuff. What do you say? What time is your break?"

"Well, the dining room has thinned out, and I don't see anyone here in the patio area except you and me. No one is coming through the doors, so I suppose I could have a break now."

"Perfect. Why don't you sit down, rest your bones, and tell me about yourself?"

"Really, not that much to tell. My story is the same as any would-be female rock band singer wanting to make it big but not able to catch a break. So, I have to make a living somehow, right? Now you, tell me about you."

"Raised in the Midwest, with down-home values. I wanted to see the world so I joined the Navy. I was always a good shot with a gun so I gave it a go with the Navy Seals. Before I knew it, I was part of the team. Now, well, I plan on finding my brother's killer."

"Earlier, I saw you talking to the customers at table twelve—Betty and Delbert. They're frequent customers here. Did you discover anything when you borrowed Delbert's magnifying glass?"

"Observant, aren't we?"

"Well, I have to keep my eyes open in case my customers need anything, don't I? Look, I want to help you catch your brother's killer. So, tell me, did you see something?"

"Fine, Penny, come closer. I want to ask you something."

She quickly sat next to Jack. Penny looked up at him and said, "Yes, ask me."

"Have you ever seen a street mime wearing a derby hat?"

"Sure, I have. Street mimes often come into the restaurant. They're nothing special. Why?"

"Have you ever heard one of them being referred to as the Jackal?"

"The Jackal? No, I can't say I have. Why? Wait, does this concern your brother, Andy? Now that I think about it, there was this time near closing. Your brother was hanging around longer than usual—that is, until he spotted something or someone from across the street. As he rushed out of here in a big hurry, I heard him say something weird or strange: 'There's a Jackal in the camp.' That's all I know. Just like that, he was gone."

"I believe this pantomimer is connected to the Romeo murders. As my brother would call him, this Jackal was the man responsible for his murder."

"No, a street mime is a serial killer? Here in my backyard?"

"Look, Penny, I've been following the story ever since it broke and—" Before the words came out of his mouth, a loud thunderclap shook the windows of the small establishment.

"Oh, I was afraid of this," Penny yelled over the loud cloudbursts that suddenly broke open.

"It's just rain. You won't melt, I promise."

"No, but I have to say it wasn't me I was thinking about. Do you have a place to stay for the night?"

"No, having arrived twelve hours ago, I haven't taken the time to arrange one—why?"

"No matter. You can stay with me. I have a couch you can sleep on, which is better than the wet sidewalks of Seattle."

"Are you sure? Penny, we've only met a few hours ago."

"Yes, I'm a pretty good judge of character, Jack. Besides, I already have your fingerprints from your beer glass on file in the back room. You don't think I would not have you investigated for a minute, would you?"

"Perfect. You're a smart cookie, aren't you?"

"Yes, I suppose I get the power of observation from my mother. Speaking of my mother, I wish I could be more honest with her."

"What do you mean by more honest?"

"Oh, it doesn't matter. Look, Jack, it's getting late, and we'll be closing in a couple of hours. Do you want to wait for me? I can drive us home."

"No—what I mean is, if it's all the same to you, could you give me your address, and I'll meet you there? Would that be all right? I would like to take this opportunity to ask those homeless guys a few questions."

"The homeless guys? Oh, you mean Robert and Patrick."

"Yeah, they're the ones, all right. You said I could find them living in a homeless community set up under the freeway overpass."

"Yes, it's lined with all manner of cardboard houses. You can't miss it. Hum, before I'd track up to the area, I'd bring a little peace offering."

"A peace offering?"

"Yeah, in the form of a bottle of booze. You'll be most welcome. Stay here; I'll get you one. You can pay me later."

Reaching into his pants, Jack said, "No, wait, here's a twenty that should cover the bottle. I still owe you for the burger."

"What I was thinking was a lot cheaper than that! Sure, I'll be right back with your purchase, sir."

Jack began to laugh after hearing Penny's response as he eyed the pedestrians walking across the street. Here and now, so close, the killer walked these very streets, looking for prey.

The only resistance came in the form of his brother. Whomever this guy was, he wasn't afraid of the cops—even when he found out Andy was watching him, catching him in his act.

Unexpectedly, there across the street was a shadow of someone walking past. Amid the people walking there, someone was wearing face paint and a derby hat.

"Shit!" Jack shouted under his breath, then stuffed

everything in his backpack and ran toward the front door.

Seeing him dart past, Penny yelled, "Jack, where are you going?"

"I saw someone across the street. I've got to go. I'll be back before you close."

"Sure, go. But why not leave your backpack with me before you do? I'll watch it for you."

"Okay. Here, take it. Look, I'll meet you back here. I must run before this street performer gets away, and l lose him."

"Fine, go. See you later. But I must warn you we're closing soon, so please hurry."

As he ran out the front door, the rain overhead began to soak him. After crossing the street, he was hampered by the many people hurrying to escape the wet conditions. He shoved through the crowds; what mattered most was finding the mime, who could not have traveled far.

"Excuse me, excuse me," Jack shouted as he shoved through the busy streets. In such a large city, he understood that many people could be dressed in black, but few wore a white painted face.

Ahead the crowds of people bunched up near the next intersection. Standing on his toes to see above everyone's heads, none of what he could see produced any derby hats in the crowd. Was he too late? "Damn," he cursed under his breath.

As he waited for the light to change, he remained focused on the intersection. Cars rushed past, driving in a hurry to get nowhere. He saw the lights from a sandwich shop reflected onto the crowd ahead.

"Excuse me," he shouted. "Must get by. Please move out of the way." The hat—he swore he saw the derby.

He didn't want to be rude, but sometimes you must, whether you like it or not. A young woman was pushed too hard, took offense, and yelled at her boyfriend to do something about it.

"Hey asshole," came the announcement.

Funny or confrontation? No matter how you want to avoid it.

"You hurt my girlfriend's arm, dumbass!"

Jack turned. "Oh, look, I'm looking for someone. I wish to apologize; truly, I do. But you must excuse me— all right?"

"No, sorry is not good enough. I'm going to kick your ass, buddy."

"No, I don't have time for this. Can we—?"

That was all that was said. He took a karate chop to the throat, and the man collapsed to the wet sidewalk, gasping for air.

Looking at the girlfriend, Jack again apologized. "He'll be okay in a few minutes. Tell him to keep breathing. His airway was only disrupted; I have to go."

With no time to waste on pleasantries, Jack hurried ahead, up another road, and waited. However, as the cars rushed past, there was no sign of the mime ahead. The light changed to green, but no one crossed, and everyone remained standing there as Jack ran across in hot pursuit of the mime.

He was surveying the area for possible sightings of the dark figure. None could be seen!

However, as fate would have it, he saw the mime walking in the opposite direction going south, half a block away.

Again, waiting for traffic to clear, Jack hurried past the slow-moving pedestrians and rushed to the next street. As he drew closer to his target, the dark figure turned around to catch a glimpse of him. Something about this street performer seemed odd; he appeared small in stature. Now with the reality of someone pursuing them, the chase was on more than ever.

No matter. Jack was determined to catch this imp and pushed through the pedestrians to get ahold of this performer. However, the more he thought about the size of the assailant, he soon realized that someone that small couldn't have killed his brother or had the strength to shove him in a dumpster. But who were they, and why were they running if they had nothing to hide?

The fact that it was night allowed the dark-clothed suspect to duck for cover. Jack lost him.

Jack saw nothing around but the obscurity of the back of the buildings. He saw trash dumpsters, filled to overflowing, and ahead a cat came shooting out of a pile of trash, screeching as it ran away with the sound of the busy street behind him. Listening, staying perfectly still, he anticipated an attack at any moment. Advancing further down the alley, he was posed much like a cat—all his reflexes attuned for retaliation if need be.

Advancing on the position, Jack called out into the darkness. "Whoever you are, I don't mean you any harm. Come out and talk to me."

No response. Nothing but silence. Jack decided to go down the alleyway. In no hurry, taking his time, Jack strolled into the darkness.

This situation was nothing new to him, thanks to his time in Afghanistan, where he worked tracking down terrorist leaders. The American streets seemed like child's play compared to that hellhole. Besides, this individual was small. Regardless of size, how much strength is required to strangle someone with a wire? Not much.

Coming to the end of the alley, Jack crossed another street and continued for some distance. Jack was about to move forward into the darkness. Stopping unexpectedly, he scratched his head and eyed the conditions around him. Having a hunch, Jack hesitated, overwhelmed with a gut feeling, something he trusted most. He turned back around for a closer look.

Jack walked up to a blue dumpster and saw something move. Posed to attack, Jack advanced. But when he was within a few feet of the dumpster, he heard a familiar clicking sound—a pistol's hammer clicking into place, ready to fire.

Jack froze.

Chapter 15

Parked on a busy street in St Paul, Minnesota, a BMW sat, waiting for its owner to appear. Down on Market Street, no one saw or paid attention to the pair of street performers slipping a note under the windshield wipers. Shortly after five o'clock, a smartly dressed woman appeared and hopped in her car. As her engine warmed up, she noticed a small envelope on the windshield, exited her car, grabbed it, and hurriedly got back inside.

Annette examined the card. It was addressed to *Dear Someone*. Thinking it strange, Annette opened the envelope and read the card.

Dear Someone,
You can't believe my luck; I've found you, at last, my pretty. Be this as you may, this is my final beckoning, no matter what you say. That the wind came out of the cloud by night, Chilling and killing my Annabel Lee.

Annette crumpled up the card and threw it on the floor of her car, fuming. As she drove home, she used her vehicle assistant to call Oliver's number and soon heard both her and Oliver's voices, saying they were busy and couldn't get to the phone, so to leave a message.

"Oliver, I don't appreciate your stupid little game of leaving a *Dear Someone* card on my car's windshield. You bastard—you think you're so damn funny. I told you that we're through. You're the one who cheated on me, remember? Please leave me alone and don't contact me again, or else I'll call the cops on you. And—for God's sake—change that stupid answering machine message, will you? Damn it, Oliver. Grow up!"

Still angered by the message and the card, Annette drove to her apartment. When she got home, she remembered a trip to the grocery store was necessary.

Frustrated, she grabbed her purse and car keys and headed back to the store. Still, she couldn't shake the feeling that Oliver was hiding in the shadows laughing at her. What a stupid game that man was playing.

How someone who graduated from Harvard with a law degree could be so immature was beyond her. They were engaged to be married this spring; all was set for the big day until the bachelor party involved a stripper.

The following day she came to his apartment early to see him nude in bed with the whore! She blamed his friend Tim, the happy bachelor, for breaking them up. She never liked the guy in the first place. But now it was all over "except for the crying," as Annette's dearly departed father would say. Nothing to be done for the once-happy couple. But why would he leave this stupid note? Unless it was Tim's idea to get back at her for breaking up with his buddy. A sick joke at best.

At the store, she exited her car and walked inside. Grabbing a grocery cart, she slowly strolled down the aisles, lost in thought. She turned down each corridor and moseyed slowly through the aisle, occasionally picking up an item and reading its list of ingredients. She dropped the item into the cart if the fat content and salt weren't too bad.

As she turned down the next aisle, she suddenly heard her name called out and turned to see a friend from her office—Kathy, along with her daughter—with a shopping cart filled to the brim.

"Amazed to see you here, Annette. I would have expected you to have a date for this evening, especially on a Friday night."

"Yeah, maybe in times past. But not now."

"Oh, sorry, I forgot about you and Oliver."

"Yes, I suppose. But it's for the best, believe me."

"Look, Madison and I aren't doing anything spectacular this evening. Why don't you come over? We'll get take-out Chinese, and we can watch a teary-eyed lovesick movie together."

"Oh, I don't know. I'm tired and thought I would turn in early this evening."

"Annette, look, I get it, but if you want to change your mind, you know my address. We'll be ordering our food when I get home."

"You know, on second thought, I think I will join you. What can I bring?"

"Wine. Red?"

"You know I recently have acquired a taste for warm sake. Have you ever had it?"

"Only once. Why? Do you want me to bring us a bottle?"

"Would you mind?"

"Not at all. It's the least I can do."

"Perfect. See you in an hour. How does that sound?"

"Great," said Kathy. Then turning to her daughter Madison, she asked her to call the Wong Foo and order their family special.

"Kathy, I don't eat that much, really."

"Oh, I'm planning for lunch the next day. No worries."

"All right, see you in a bit. Bye."

Annette was off and hurried home. When she arrived at her apartment, she quickly put the groceries away and freshened up. She left her apartment and remembered that she had agreed to buy a bottle of sake.

She stopped at the liquor store near Kathy's house. She was in and out within a matter of minutes. Having been to Kathy's home only once, she struggled with which streets to turn down.

She remembered her house was on a busy street and thought it was off Jefferson Ave. But when she drove down the road, nothing looked familiar. The houses all looked older, probably built during the 1950s. She was sure Kathy's house was much newer, say around the 1980s, but nothing was familiar to her.

Pulling into an abandoned gas station parking lot, she grabbed her purse, opened a zipper, pulled out her cell phone, and ran down the list of contacts. When she came across Kathy's number, she selected her number and waited.

As the phone rang, something in the shadows moved near the back of the building. As she watched, she saw a lone figure emerge from the darkness.

"Annette, don't tell me you changed your mind?"

Watching the strange figure and wanting to get out of there, she responded, "No, no. Listen, I'm lost. I stopped at an abandoned gas station; everywhere I look, it's all run-down buildings."

"Oh, you must have gone south on Jefferson. Turn back around and travel north about five miles. You can't miss us. We're next to the school."

"Yes, okay, see you soon. Bye." She hung up and glanced over to where the stranger was lurking—and, to her surprise, he was gone.

But when she turned to drive away, she saw, to her horror, the man was looking at her from the driver's side window.

"Get away from me!" Annette screamed out, then shoved her car into gear and drove away, squealing her tires.

Shaken, she arrived at Kathy's house looking disturbed.

"Are you all right, Annette? What happened to you?"

"Oh, you can't believe my luck. When I pulled over to call you from that abandoned gas station to ask you where you lived, someone crawled out of the shadows. When I hung up they were standing near my driver's car door. I didn't know what they wanted and didn't hang around to find out. I screamed to get away and tore out of there as quickly as possible."

"Come in. Hurry. You will feel better once you're around friends, so come in quickly and get comfortable."

The smell of Chinese food filled the place with a pleasant aroma. Unfortunately, having been scared, Annette was in no mood to eat.

"Annette, sit yourself down. We can eat whenever you want.
I already told Madison to go ahead and eat. Are you sure you're, okay?"

"Oh, I'll be fine. But truthfully, I cannot get that guy's image out of my head."

"Annette, have you ever seen him before?"

"Heavens no, how could I? I've never been to this part of town before. I've only traveled here to see you. Besides, what's the luck of me running into someone like that? Who could guess the odds of me stopping at that particular place in time and there being Mitch or Randy, old school chums from another life? Damn it, Kathy, I have no clue who that guy was."

"I know. Around the city, the homeless population is growing at an alarming rate. Ever since this damn Covid crap, everyone's lives have been disrupted one way or another."

"Hey, before I forget—the wine! Here you go." She handed Kathy the bottle wrapped in a paper bag.

Taking the bottle and unscrewing the cap, Kathy said, "Yes, I believe at a time as this, a glass is in order!"

"You said it, sister. I agree!"

"So, do you like your sake chilled or warm?"

"Warm, you say? Most of the wine I ever tasted was chilled white wine. I'll tell you what. If it's no trouble, let me try mine warmed."

"No trouble at all. I have everything ready."

A short time later, after filling two glasses, Kathy joined her guest at the counter and sat in the opposite chair. After taking a sip, she said, "Hum, I like. I didn't look at the label. What type of sake is this?" she said while swirling the liquid in the glass.

"It's a Kubota Manju Junmai Daiginjo Sake."

"I like the richness of the flavor. Good choice! Now, Annette, is there anything else you want to talk about? I know this breakup with Oliver wasn't easy."

"No, that's for sure. It wasn't, but I did what I had to do.
I couldn't marry someone who cheated on me so easily in a moment of weakness. Alcohol was only part of the problem. I realized that Oliver was a happy bachelor when I met him. No, a guy like that should stay single. He could never be faithful. It's not in him. But there we go, us females thinking that we can change a man—right?"

"Yes, I suppose. But then there are women like myself who became a widow much too young in life and had no choice but to be lonely. Yes, I did the dating thing for a while. But after you've had the best, no one can ever fit the mold again."

"No, Kathy, I believe you'll find someone when you least expect it."

"Maybe. Listen, all this food isn't going to eat itself. What do you say, would you like some?"

"You know, now that you mention it, I believe it's time we enjoy a bite or two."

Kathy took down some plates from the cupboard and opened the white cartons from the box. After filling the plate with some fried rice and General Lee orange chicken, then adding an egg roll, she handed it to Annette.

But before Annette took a bite, she looked at Kathy, her expression one of concern, and said, "Something happened to me earlier that seemed weird. I found a note on my car windshield when I got off work. After I read it, I crumpled it up and threw it inside my car."

"What do you mean? What was in it?"

"Something stupid that Oliver wrote to frighten me. I know he was upset about the breakup—even more, because his mother was disappointed that he couldn't keep his pants on.

"I heard from the grapevine that there was some talk about how she cut him out of her will. I can't say whether that's true, but can you imagine being cut from his mother's will and made to stand on his own?

"I know he used to talk a lot about what he would do when his mother kicked the bucket and how he would spend all that money. Of fundamental importance, and what mattered most, was the need to have grandchildren. And now no grandchildren, no money—poor Oliver!"

"Do you still have the note in your car?"

"Sure, I guess. Why?"

"I'd like to read it."

"Why?"

"Please. Could you just indulge me and get the note?"

"You promise not to take a bite of my delicious food?"

"Okay. Come on, hurry."

"Sure, I'll be right back."

As Annette disappeared outside, a nagging concern shadowed Kathy, and she became frightened of the prospect that her friend could become a victim of the Romeo murders. When she returned, Kathy eagerly asked to see the little card. When Annette handed it to her, she was taken aback by the seriousness her friend displayed.

"Here, take it. It doesn't mean anything—not really, just a hoax played out by Oliver, I assure you."

After reading the small card, Kathy's interest was piqued, and she looked up at her friend. "I'm not so sure. I just read the card to see what it said. It could be genuine, but only the police could tell. Here, I think you should call the law enforcement agency or at least drop by the station and give them the card.

"Although if it's booked as evidence, it will have both of our fingerprints all over it. But it does remind me of the Romeo murders in Seattle."

"Why? As I told you before, it's a prank played by Oliver. You don't know how pissed he was at me! You know, this situation reminds me of another story. I had a friend many years ago, although it seemed like yesterday. Anyway, it was during the AIDS epidemic. She started dating this guy she met at a club. At first, all was great, but after a couple of months, the guy got scared and wanted to break it off. Who knows why, but my friend Brenda was heartbroken at first. But then she wanted revenge on the guy for breaking her heart!"

"What happened?"

"For the guy, the worst scenario imaginable. That bitch wrote an anonymous letter saying that one of her sex partners had contracted AIDS, so he should get tested immediately."

"Damn, that's harsh."

"No kidding. Playing around with a death sentence just because the guy broke up with you? So, you see, this foolish game of love and hate is not for the weak-hearted. Could lose millions. No wonder he wants to hurt me!" So, in my case, it's Oliver."

"I see what you mean. But still, I'd deliver it to the police."

"Let me ask you a question: The Romeo killings, weren't they in Seattle? Hello!"

"Annette, don't be such a smart ass, okay? I'm your friend, and I would hate to see something bad happen to you."

"No, I get it. I do, and I want to thank you for your concern. But I'll be fine. Hey, look, our food is getting cold. Let's have a glass of warm sake, okay? Alcohol always calms my nerves."

"Mine, too. But are you sure you don't want to call the police?"

"No, really. Everything will be all right. The truth is Oliver is such a sissy that he wouldn't be the one that put the card on my car. He probably hired someone to do his dirty work."

"You know him better than anyone, I suppose. Just make me a promise: When you get home tonight, you'll call me, okay?"

"Of course, I will."

"Let's have some sake. What do you say?"

"Works for me."

Annette wanted to see a favorite movie on Showtime, and all the worries about the card were soon forgotten. After they ate, both Annette and Kathy got comfortable on the couch. But halfway through the romantic love scene,

Kathy paused the movie and asked, "Annette, you don't know anyone that would want to hurt you?"

"What? Why would you ask me that?"

"I can't get that damn card out of my mind. I keep thinking, what if?" Kathy argued.

"What if what? We've worked together for how long now, six or seven years? Have you ever known me to be cruel or hateful toward anyone? Have you ever heard me say anything to reveal prejudice or some such nonsense?"

"No, I can't say I have. No, nothing like that."

"But Annette, please tell me, have you ever pissed anyone off from your past? You know, someone that— well, for no other words—wants to kill you?"

"Shit. You know, Kathy, you're acting strange and weird. I cannot believe you sometimes."

"No—really, you could tell me. Has there ever been someone who has told you: 'I want you dead?'

Annette took a long breath. The change in her friend's demeanor was becoming tiresome at best. "Look, Kathy, no one has ever said anything like that to me. I'm a good person, but now you are upsetting me. I can't help it; there are weirdos in the world! Shit, I ran into one this evening trying to find your place. I'm sure that guy would have killed me or worse if given the opportunity. But no one—I mean…" She trailed off.

"What?"

"Oh, it's silly. Nothing, really. I can't blame Bridget McBride for saying she wanted to see me dead. After all, it was an accident; she knows that!"

"What accident?"

"Bridget's father, my stepfather, Chester McBride, was accidentally hit by a truck and pinned to a tree— crushed to death."

"Oh, my heavens, your stepsister. It was her father you

killed?"

"Damn it, yes. I was the driver. Regrettably, I was eager to learn how to drive. One Saturday morning, I thought everyone was gone, so I felt free to start up Chester's truck and practice my driving skills. Sadly, I wasn't alone with my friend Katie.

"Almost on a dare, as I was bragging about teaching myself how to drive. Katie egged me on. As if to show off my driving skills, I thought it would be fun to burn the tires. When I did, the truck shot forward like a rocket and soon lost control. As the vehicle left the driveway, I thought it was better to turn around and park it. But I was wrong. I was still traveling at a high rate of speed. So, when I turned, the truck veered toward the tree where Chester was raking up some leaves. The rest is history."

"What did the police say?"

"Well, the district attorney was my uncle on my mother's side. No charges were ever filed."

"Oh, I see!"

"No, actually, you do not! Sadly, my mother, Chester's second wife, was cunning and astute. At the time, no one would have suspected her dealings concerning Chester's will. But months before, dear old Mommy had changed Chester's will and removed Bridget, his only daughter, from receiving any inheritance."

"Oh shit. No wonder you feel nervous."

"No, not even close. Yes, at the time, she swore to kill me, but that was well over ten years ago. Besides, she lives in Portland, Oregon, the last I heard. Yes, I realize she has an ax to grind, but it wasn't my idea; it was my mother's. I'm only guilty by association."

"Annette, you better have another drink."

"You know what? If it's all the same to you, can we make this another night? I feel the sake isn't sitting too well—if you know what I mean?"

"What! You're leaving already?"

"Yeah, I'm sorry. But all this talk and emotions about Chester's death is getting to me—admittedly more than I thought it would."

"Well, I understand. We'll have to make it another time. Promise me you'll take some food with you to eat later if you feel better."

"Yes, of course. Again, I'm sorry, Kathy, for ruining your evening."

"No, not even close. Besides, I've seen that movie a hundred times before. He's already dead."

"Who? Don't tell me. Not the main character?"

"Yeah, I'm afraid so."

"Damn it, Kathy, thanks for ruining it for me. Shit, he's already dead? Damn, I wanted to see that movie but not now."

"Here, let me prepare a plate to take with you. We'll plug in the movie the next time you drop by. It has a great ending; his son comes back to life!"

"His son is alive? Damn it, on second thought, watch something you haven't seen before. How's that sound?"

"Great, I can't wait!"

After gathering her things, Annette walked out of the apartment carrying a goodie bag of food—more than she'd ever be able to eat on her own. On her way home, she could not shake the memory of Chester's death. That morning so many years ago was something she tried to forget. But bam, there it was again.

She recalled the funeral and all the crying, Bridget's slap across her face, the sting from her hand, and Bridget's screams when she discovered her father's money was gone—maybe not gone but tied up. She also thought about the day she and her mother met in the lawyer's office.

When Annette arrived at her apartment, she felt tired even though it was shortly past eight o'clock. All the emotions and heartache from the breakup left her in a depressive state. Sleep was the best cure. When she unlocked her front door and walked inside, a gentle breeze from the north lifted the curtains near the patio door. Flicking on a light, she set down her purse and keys and locked the door behind her.

In her bedroom, she changed her clothes and slipped on a cotton outfit as her sleepwear. Still feeling the effects of the sake, she felt lethargic, much like a slug, as she strolled along.

At that time, a thought occurred to her. In a hurry to get home, she realized she had left the note back at Kathy's apartment. *Damn, I wanted to read that card again. Oh well, I'll call Kathy tomorrow and ask her to bring it to work with her on Monday.* The card was meant for her and her alone.

Over toward the sliding door, she heard someone giggling. Next, she felt a cold, metal noose wrapped around her throat from behind and tightened.

Struggling to free herself, she reached behind to dig out the eyes of her strangler. As she fought and kicked to be free, a figure appeared out of the shadows near the door, dressed as a street mime.

The vile character approached while Annette fought to get free. Not to be ignored in this fight to stay alive, she kicked and jumped, about to free herself from the grip killing her. Unbelievably, the other individual unexpectedly broke out in laughter.

This person crept close and swayed about with excitement—with a smile on their face, enjoying the show.

Her fight and resolve to save herself diminished with each passing second.

"Did you think for one second, I'd forget what you did? Could you, Annette, ever imagine yourself free to wed and live happily ever after?"

Annette reached out to scratch the mime's face, but the mime was too far away. Digging her fingernails into the mime's neck, she hoped to pull the wire away from cutting off her airway. But it was of no use. The attacker, who held her life in their hands, gripped the wire and tightened their grip even more.

"You fool, did you ever consider your fiancé—poor Oliver—was innocent of cheating on you? That morning you found him in bed with a stripper? There was no stripper but me!"

In the last seconds of Annette's life, a horrible reality unfolded as the mime unexpectedly began rubbing off the white face paint. Then, as she feared, Annette could see that the figure before her was her half-sister Bridget.

With the help of some sick-minded monster holding the steel wire, Annette's life was fading. What possible argument could she retort?

"Finally, I shall have my revenge upon you, bitch. Look at what you've done to my father. Die, you fucking bitch. Die and rot in hell for what you've done to me! The bitter taste of revenge tastes sweet in my mouth."

Reaching out desperately, Annette wanted more than anything to get her hands on her stepsister. But this attempt was short-lived as everything around her began to darken. She collapsed in the arms of her attacker. Her life was over.

Her last thought was of Oliver and his cries of innocence.

Chapter 16

"Don't shoot the bastard!" came a man's voice from the shadows.

"I wouldn't shoot an unarmed man. No worries. Keep your hands where I can see them, mister," came a female voice.

Jack turned to look to his right. He saw the tiny figure dressed as a mime, all in black—hard to make out except for the white painted face. The stainless-steel gun was now clearly visible.

"Listen, you two, if it's money you want, I'm afraid you're shit out of luck. I don't have much on me. Sorry, you'll have to buy your drugs from someplace else!"

"Drugs? Who said anything about drugs?" the man replied.

"Tell me now, what's this all about?" Jack shouted back.

"No, wait, I'm the one holding the gun. You tell me why you're following me, buddy!"

"Simple. You remind me of someone I wanted to speak with, that's all," Jack answered, lowering his arms to his side.

"Get 'em up. Don't make me shoot you!" the woman yelled back.

"Look, what's this all about? I told you I don't have any money. I explained that I mistakenly thought you were someone else. If you want to shoot me, then go ahead. It's not like I haven't had a gun pointed at me before. Besides, if you shoot me, there will be a military investigation. And, believe me, the government will hunt you down for killing a decorated Navy Seal!"

"You're a Navy Seal? How do we know that's true and you're not a murderer, a special kind of killer that strangles a woman? Tell us, huh? How are we supposed to know you're telling the truth?" said the woman.

"I have my identification card here in my wallet."

"Antonne, please be a gentleman and check the guy's identification. If he tries some funny business, I'll keep my gun pointed at him."

"Now, you listen to me, girl. Make sure you don't shoot me by accident," said Antonne. "Do you hear me now?"

"Yes, yes, go on. I have my eye on him."

From behind the trash dumpster, Antonne approached slowly while Jack kept his arms above his head. Unknown to these novices, Jack had trained for situations like this in combat. Without blinking his eye, Jack turned and had Antonne within his grasp, threatening to snap his neck if the woman didn't drop her gun. Left with little choice, she laid her weapon on the wet asphalt and stepped away.

Releasing the large man, Jack swooped down and picked up the .38 revolver before anyone could resist.

"Get over here now!" Jack ordered.

The mime came into the light, a tiny figure dressed in black wearing white face makeup, complete with dark tears running down her cheeks.

"Now, tell me, what's this all about?"

Looking over at the large man, the girl said, "Me and Antonne were out to catch someone. A dangerous man who killed before, here in the city. A strangler, someone the police have deemed the Romeo Strangler."

"Oh—I see. Here, please take your gun back. I won't be needing it."

"What? You're not going to shoot us?" Antonne responded.

"Why on earth would I shoot you guys? Besides, I'm also looking for that same son of a bitch. He's the guy the police have said killed my brother, Andy."

"The strangler killed your brother? That doesn't make any sense. From what I know, he's only interested in killing women," the girl responded, appearing from the darkness as she reached down to pick up her gun.

"Why—or how, I should say—in the hell do you know so much about the killer?"

"It's simple. I've seen him."

"Okay, how did you see him and survive?"

"He was out to kill me! I was one of those women that got a stupid note on my car. He was waiting in my apartment. That man was waiting in my apartment to strangle me!"

"Oh, I see. Yes, it is beginning to make perfect sense. Tell me what he looks like."

"Oh my God, your worst nightmare. All this happened some months back when I lived in Seattle. Stupid me didn't have a clue back then that I was on this killer's radar. I lived my life as though nothing was wrong or could go wrong. Until that day, I only worried about what I would wear to work. That day my world changed, and when I looked into that monster's eyes, I knew I had to do something to stop him before he killed again."

"You're stupid if for one minute you think you'll ever catch this guy with a gun. Really, what are you thinking?"

"We caught you, didn't we?"

"Fine. What do you plan to do? Shoot his balls off?"

"I've had intense training since leaving Seattle. The

police and the FBI haven't been able to catch this killer. I alone have seen him. When we meet again, I'll know it's him."

Turning to the man, Jack said, "What's your story, buddy? How did you get roped into this mess?"

"I was kind of a friend of your brother's. Often when it was raining outside—I mean raining hard—I would leave the back room open for your brother to have a place to sleep for the night. I liked Andy; you could say we shared stories of the war, although fighting in different theaters—mine was during Vietnam and his in Desert Storm."

"Thank you, Antonne, for showing my brother kindness as you did. We encouraged him to come home, but he wouldn't. Still, to this day, I don't know why."

"My name is Patricia Harper. What did you say your name was?"

"Jack McIntyre."

"Hello. Again, I'm sorry about your brother."

"Thank you, and I'm sorry you were almost strangled to death. Look, I'm not from here. Is there someplace we can talk and get out of the weather?"

"Yes, the Tin Cup is only a few blocks away. Let's go there. I can't say it will still be open by the time we arrive," Antonne replied.

"You mean go and see Penny?"

"Oh, so you've met Penny, have you?" Patricia asked.

"Yes, I have. Let's go there before the restaurant closes."

"I'll lead the way. I know a shortcut," Antonne announced.

When they arrived at the Tin Cup, it was dark, as if the restaurant had closed and everyone had left for home. An unexpected car horn beeped. The small group turned to see a foreign compact. There in the driver's seat was Penny.

She approached them and said, "It took you long enough. I didn't think you were coming back!" she announced to Jack.

"Well, I was delayed, you could say."

"Yeah, I thought he was the Romeo Strangler, and I held my gun on him and would not let him leave," Patricia said.

"Who? Jack?" Penny asked.

"Hey, the guy was following me, and I thought it was the strangler. How was I to know?"

"What now?" Antonne asked.

"While I waited for Jack to show up, business slowed to a crawl so I asked for the rest of the night off. Janey agreed to cover the rest of my shift. Let's go to my place; it seems we have a lot to talk about, don't we?"

Turning to Patricia, Jack announced, "Before I get into a car with this girl, I want to be sure that her gun is pointing in the other direction. What do you say, Patricia?"

"I still have the safety on. No worries. Hey, Jack, listen to me a moment, damn it. You didn't see that son of a bitch. I did, and I must say it wasn't a picnic. Tell me, Jack, have you ever stared into the eyes of a killer?"

"Not only a cold-blooded killer but the barrel of a gun the man was holding."

"Okay, let's put aside our feelings. It won't get us anywhere if we can't get along," Penny announced.

"Yes, you're right. I get it! Let's try this another way."

Sticking out his hand, he said, "Hello, Patricia and Antonne. My name is Jack McIntyre."

"Hello, Jack, I'm glad to know you, brother."

"Yes, me, too. Hello, Jack," Patricia said grudgingly.

With everyone united, they quickly became colleagues in one cause, piled into the small car, and headed to Penny's place. When they arrived, everyone treaded up the wooden stairway to the second-story apartment.

Soon corks were popping, and drinks flowed. That night it was discovered that Jack had recently been discharged from the Navy. Before he returned home, he wanted to solve his brother's murder if he could. Being new to the city, he didn't understand how events there were played out.

Regardless of the stories told that evening, none seemed more affected in wanting to see the Romeo strangler captured than Patricia. None except Antonne had heard her describe what had happened that night. Having drunk enough to loosen her tongue, she recalled the events of that evening so many months ago.

She felt safe in the back of the police cruiser. The wet rain dripped off the police car's windows. Then appearing out of the shadows was the hideous face of the killer, her killer. She remembered all the details—how that monster was waiting in her apartment to murder her.

Everyone, a captured audience, listened to Patricia's description when she returned home to her parent's house and how she felt as if she had abandoned the strangler's following targets. She couldn't live with herself if another life was lost and wanted to find a way to prevent it.

Patricia said, "That's when I asked for his help, and Antonne agreed to help me catch the strangler."

"Patricia, did you ever consider that you could still be the next victim of the strangler? Foolish girl, why would you ever think that by dressing like a mine, you would catch this guy? If you continue, I believe you will die for your troubles. This man is ruthless and daring by all accounts. I've talked to Detective Stevens. He described to me what happened back in your apartment, how the strangler killed his last victim, a guy you might have known, who was in the wrong place at the right time."

"What guy are you talking about? What guy I must know?"

"Haven't you heard? Didn't you know that someone else was murdered in your apartment? Some young guy was found inside your apartment with a kitchen knife jabbed in his eye!"

"No, no, I didn't hear anything about that. When I thought it was a joke, I ran for my life. Then this guy showed up and asked me out! Oh my God, someone—" She paused. "Wait, someone else was there? Was it the guy who asked me out on a date? His name was Robbie. Do you think it was him, the guy? I mean, shit, of course, it was him. I just never knew!"

Hearing the news of someone being killed in her apartment made Patricia upset. She began to cry and whispered, "I never knew!"

"Look, no doubt the FBI has investigators searching for the killer. Not to mention the police are out looking for this guy. Now listen to me, everyone. Let's give this some thought! What do we know so far?"

"That's simple. A mime tried to murder me. Damn, I don't know this freak, but he was in my apartment wanting to strangle me to death!" Patricia cried.

"Yes, at your apartment complex was where my brother, Andy, died. But besides him, another guy was murdered named Robbie."

"Who else? I mean, who else has been murdered by this strangler?" Penny announced.

"The newspapers mentioned this man strangled at least two other women," Antonne said.

Jack's cell phone began ringing. Removing it from his pants pocket, he looked to see who the caller was, then said, "Excuse me, will you?

"Hello, this is Jack. Yes, hello, Detective Stevens.

Sorry I didn't get back to you—what is that you're saying? Another Romeo murder—where? St. Paul, Minnesota!"

Covering his phone, Jack looked at the group and said, "There's been another Romeo murder!"

Jack continued talking on the phone and asked, "What's that, Stevens? The victim's friend said she had a note delivered to her car. This note changes things a bit. Okay, thanks for the info. We'll be in touch. Stevens, before you go—why call me? Oh, I see. Yes, of course. Goodbye."

Turning to see the shocked expressions around the room, Jack said, "Can you believe it? Another murder, except this time our killer has been on tour across the country."

Penny remarked, "Wow, that does change things, doesn't it?"

"Just a little. Who would have ever thought this guy would travel nationwide?" Patricia sobbed.

"None of us—no, none would suspect. After hearing this latest news, I have realized this killer can never be caught—nope, no way," Jack said.

Suddenly, the room grew still, and no one spoke.

Out of the blue, Penny confessed, "I have seen this mime before. He would stand across the street and hide in the shadows. When something or someone sparked his interest, the killer would go into his little performance, offering ugly flowers to the ladies, or he'd break out in a little dance—all the while holding out his derby hat for the spectators to deposit some change. Usually, not much was in the way of monetary worth. Afterward, he'd storm off and disappear. Damn, he was right in front of me, and I didn't know it—the strangler, I mean, it had to be him. That guy always gave me the creeps, I can tell you!"

"I've read many books on serial killers, and one thing

usually rings true: They're opportunists!" said Jack. "Besides this, they have hunting grounds where they feel safe and, most often, easy access to escape. When you study Jack the Ripper, you'll find that he didn't travel any farther than the Whitechapel district, the east side of London. Usually, places such as these were where the prostitutes conducted their business."

"Yes, that's true, Jack. But don't forget, we've had men like Dellmus Colvin, AKA The Interstate Strangler, who claimed to have killed forty-seven to fifty women on the open road," Antonne proclaimed.

Grabbing a tissue from the coffee table, Patricia remarked, "Antonne, I thought you were just a cook. Is there something you haven't been telling us?"

"Why is it that people judge you on your occupation in life without considering one's past experiences? Do you all believe I've been a cook all my life? No, I'm proud to say I was once a police sergeant for the Seattle Police department! I was injured in a shootout about ten years ago. I'm only here because I heard about what happened to Patricia. You see, I live in the same complex that she once lived in, and I was downstairs at the time of Robbie's murder, watching the investigation unfold. I remember you running up to Detective Stevens, calling him a stupid bastard for sending you up to your apartment alone. Patricia, think about it. Do you remember the day I called you at your parents' home?"

"Yes. You said something about attending a victim's seminar!"

"That's right. But you insisted that the killer must be caught by any means necessary, even offering to act as bait to catch the strangler. Somehow you convinced me that you were ready to help me track down the strangler, saying you saw him once before and knew what he looked like!"

"Yes. But again, I thought you were working with a special victim's organization or something like that! I explained that I had just finished firearms training and could protect myself if necessary."

"Yeah, about that. I'm glad you didn't shoot my ass," Jack remarked.

"No worries. I wasn't aiming for your ass, Jack."

"Oh, that doesn't sound good."

"So how do you two expect to catch the Romeo Strangler?" Penny asked.

Antonne finished his glass and sat it on the table next to him. "The idea was to spark an interest in seeing Patricia dressed as a mime. To me, the killer would naturally be curious at seeing another mine such as himself and follow her. When he appeared in the designated place, we would spring the trap, then have the strangler arrested. Then the world would be safer!"

"Hey, you two, did you ever consider what would happen to Patricia if the killer got ahold of her? I mean, if he strangled her to death?" Jack asked.

"That would never have happened—believe me, she was in no danger. I was never out of eye contact. Even when Jack followed her, I had my eye on both of them the entire time. Plus, lest we forget, I'm armed!" Antonne explained.

"Oh, and, lest you forget, I had you in a chokehold!" Jack laughed.

"You were lucky, man. I had you where I wanted you the whole time."

"Well, it seems painfully apparent that the killer has moved on. So, what now?" Penny asked.

"Good question. All I know is that I'm not traveling to St. Paul, Minnesota. This situation sucks—the whole dynamics have changed. I mean, who is this creep anyway?

Why go to Minnesota—what's the attraction?" Jack asked.

"Shit, man, it could be for any number of reasons: an old girlfriend, getting married. A revenge killing—again, involving a past relationship—but it's getting late," Antonne said.

"Jack, why did Stevens call you to tell you about the Romeo murder?" Patricia questioned.

"It's quite simple, really. The detective wanted me to stop looking for the guy who killed my brother. He felt compelled to tell me about the murder in St. Paul so I wouldn't go around harassing the locals—I suppose, either way, there's nothing for me here now; I imagine I'll be leaving Seattle soon."

"I agree with Antonne; it's getting late. I have the early shift at the Tin Cup and must go to bed. Jack that offer is still available if you want to sleep on the couch."

"I do. I mean, yes, thank you."

"So, what about you two? Do you have a place to sleep?"

"Ever since I arrived, I've been staying at my old boyfriend's condo. He's trying his best to make amends and has allowed me the bed while he sleeps on the couch," Patricia announced.

"Hey, you all need not worry about me. I have my loft above the Tin Cup," Antonne remarked.

"Okay. If I may, I have a suggestion: Let's meet for breakfast at the Tin Cup. I'll even pick up the tab," Penny said.

"Wow, all this. A place to sleep and breakfast," Jack said with a chuckle.

Antonne remarked, "We just brought in some delicious hams from the Netherlands—honey baked if I recall. Listen, don't none of you forget, I'm the cook. I'll fix you all up proper."

Penny's cell phone rang. "I wonder who that could be?"

To her dismay, it was her mother calling. "Mom, it's not Tuesday. Why are you calling me so late? What? What do you mean I've been lying to you? Mom—Mother, wait, I have company. I can't get into this right now—let me call you back in the morning! What do you mean you want me back home in Portland? Why? What's that? No college. About that, Mom—what? The Romeo Strangler is now living in Portland? Mom, why would you say that? You've seen him—how? What do you mean there's something else? You say the killer is in love?"

Chapter 17

Those murderers live among us, unsuspecting humans. It's up to them if they choose to reveal themselves. They decide when to kill. It's up to them entirely—a desperate uncalculating desire to feel a life drain from the warm body.

Many weeks after arriving in St. Paul, Harland enjoyed a cigarette in bed after having sex. He busied himself with thoughts of his life and how much things had changed.

To him, living an ordinary existence in society meant he could easily hide among the unsuspecting fools, almost as easily as a cattle rancher who surveys the four-footed steaks within his corral.

Something he found most troubling was the circumstance involving his girlfriend Bridget McBride and her taste for blood; she liked it—a lot! He was anxious to kill again, and her request to find their next target was most bothersome.

He couldn't get his last encounter with the fortune teller out of his mind and the audacity she displayed that day, telling him it wasn't her time to die and that she was to perish in her bed, not at his hands. More than anything, he wanted to prove her wrong.

Caution and attentiveness were paramount. It was the only reason Harland wasn't rotting in prison somewhere. Sadly, he realized he exposed himself to being discovered by allowing Bridget to indulge in his little game of killing.

A conundrum indeed for him. It would be a simple matter of killing Bridget to keep her quiet, and his concerns would be dealt with efficiently at the end of a wire. But to kill the woman who stole his heart? Even in his most deplorable state of mind, he could never hurt this angel of mercy.

Bridget appeared in the room, partly naked, with a towel wrapped around her head, wearing panties, and bare-chested. She took a drag after she removed the cigarette from his lips, exhaled, smiled, and walked back into the bathroom.

Still somewhat tired from the long drive to St. Paul, Harland didn't move and listened to Bridget break out into song, a child's melody, something he hadn't heard since childhood. But now, hearing it sung by the female voice, the words that brought him such pain evoked a memory of long ago. Harland's thoughts drifted to when he was a child.

His only sister, Harlow, two years older than himself, used to sing that same song when she would often put him to bed—most often hungry.

Harlow—fuck, he hadn't thought of her in years. The motive behind the hate! Such hate is strong enough to kill. Harlow, his older sister, was always fighting off the drunk sons of bitches trying to rape her. Their lives together revolved around their alcoholic mother, who didn't care. Harlow's suicide at age thirteen was her only way out of the situation.

Reappearing in the room, combing her hair, Bridget asked, "So what do you have planned today? Anything fun?"

"Yes, let me ask you a question: Ever had your fortune been told?"

"No, I don't believe in that shit."

"You might start to believe after today. Anyway, I have something fun that I believe you will enjoy. Today we're—I mean *you*—will be visiting a fortune teller."

"Oh really?"

"Yes. I'm curious to know if any of her predictions are accurate."

"What predictions?"

"One is predicting the fortune teller's death, of course!"

"Oh, goody gum drops. Sounds like fun to me."

"Fun, yes, for me, too."

***

Just before closing, a young girl stood on the busy sidewalk outside Madam Miko's place of business. Hesitant to enter, she stalked back and forth, glancing inside the glass window. At the time, Cassia was dusting her ceramic figurines, watching.

In a sudden change of heart, the girl walked up to the door and opened it, stepping inside.

Madam Mikos said, "Hello, may I help you?"

"Please help me. I've never done this type of thing before, you understand. But I'm desperate for help. You are my last option."

"Yes. Please come inside, and have a seat."

Following Cassia to a small room, the girl acted strangely; this of its own accord was nothing new. Most of her clients were nervous. But this stranger wore a blackness around her as if a thick black cloud hung atop her head.

"Please sit down and make yourself comfortable. I would like to ask you a few questions before we begin."

"Whatever you want, go ahead. I'm an open book."

Taking a chair across from her proposed client, Cassia picked up some Tarot cards and slowly shuffled them.

Then she began to draw out cards from the deck and laid them down on the table.

"Please, tell me, what help can I offer you today? You spoke of being desperate. What type of assistance do you need, young lady?"

"My father died in a horrible accident. Before his death, he often spoke of a treasure of gold coins he kept hidden away for me, and when I grew up, he promised that I would receive them for my inherence. Sadly, he was killed by some bitch who couldn't drive a car! I've about given up on ever finding the treasure until I came across your shop. Are you truly a fortune teller?"

"Hum, yes. Some say I have been blessed with foresight, able to see into the past and future. But I say it's all hidden from us, this world beyond the curtain. We only receive small glimpses into that other world and nothing else."

"Still, if you are not some crackpots out to steal old ladies' social security checks, you might be able to help me. Tell me, what do you see when you lay down those Tarot cards? Does it unlock any secrets? Can you see the real me?"

"No! You are a bit of a mystery. It seems your glow is clouded; the cards are confusing to me right now. I am sorry, but I cannot help you."

"Wait, don't say that. Wait, what about your crystal ball, the one in the center of the table? Tell me, will that help you find the answers I seek?"

"I cannot say. Yes, perhaps in times past, I have used the properties of the crystal as a way to focus my attention. But truthfully—I'm not too flippy on you! You're hiding something; there is something about you—you have sinister intent, and I cannot place my finger on it. Maybe your indecisiveness is throwing off my senses. But whatever it is, I do not like your aura or dissemination."

"No, lady, you have me all wrong! All I want is to find my father's chest of gold and nothing more."

"I can see your lips moving, but I do not believe your words! You're up to something, and I do not like it!"

"You cannot be real. You're a fake like the others I've met. If you were the real thing, you'd know that my only wish is to find what is mine. I knew you couldn't help me. You're nothing but a charlatan, like all the rest!"

"I beg your pardon, young lady! You don't know the extent of my powers. There is one man alone who knows that my gifts are real. He and I have spoken recently. Sterling has warned me of a stranger at my door promising to be something they're not. Promising to be innocent, but in truth, the stranger is here to murder me! Tell me, child, are you she, the killer at my door?"

Suddenly, the young woman cried with sobbing tears running down her cheeks. She cupped her face into her palms and said, "How could I ever be a killer? I'm innocent of murdering anyone. Please, look into your crystal ball there—if you must search out the truth and see if what I'm telling you isn't legitimate. Oh my God, who will help me if you won't? I have asked so many people to help me find my father's treasure, but no one has been able to. They're all fakes, every last one of them! If I can't find it, I might as well kill myself!"

"Child, there's no need for such words. I will help you. But before I can, I must prepare myself. I must prepare the room by dimming the lights, closing the curtains, and lighting the necessary number of candles in the room. For now, you remain here, and when I return, we will begin to communicate with the departed spirits. Now please—this is important—you must give me some time to meditate and prepare myself. Otherwise, I will not be able to focus on the other world. Can you do this for me?"

"Certainly. In the meantime, I shall meditate as well. Hopefully, by concentrating on my father, I can help you, or I can help myself find the treasure he intended to leave me."

"Yes, that's a great idea. I'll soon return, and we can begin. Hum, there is just a little matter of the offering. Normally, I wouldn't bring it up. But we must pay our taxes, and business has been down because of the Covid thing, you understand?"

"I expected this. Remember, I have sought out others in an attempt to discover my father's treasure. Usually, for their troubles, I write a check for five hundred dollars. Tell me, will that be sufficient?"

"Oh, yes, thank you. I'll soon return so we can begin. Afterward, if we discover the truth and are satisfied, you can pay me what you feel our session was worth. I'm optimistic, aren't you?"

"Yes. I have never felt so close to fulfilling my destiny."

"I will be back soon. Take this time to relax. Now listen, you must promise me that this suicide nonsense will never be thought of again. Promise me!"

"I do, I promise. It's just that when I feel desperate with no hope of ever finding what my father left me, I get overwhelmed and want to end it all."

"After today, I 'm sure you will have all the answers you seek."

"I'm sure I will."

"Now allow me time to concentrate. I'll be back soon."

"Perfect. Can't wait."

Cassia went into her bedroom and began to disrobe. She removed her blouse and tossed it on the bed. Reaching inside her closet, she pulled out a familiar black silk smock decorated with fine stitching, depicting the stars and other celestial bodies.

She sat on a pillow on the floor and crossed her legs. Taking her fingertips, she softly tapped them together. Clearing her mind, she concentrated on the stranger in the next room.

Within her spirit, this was proving to be complicated—a lot of confusion and mixed noise. More and more, she narrowed her attention to the girl alone. Darkness invaded her thoughts. Something unclear—her motives, her reasons for the visit today. A flash there, a moment of happiness. Yes, something in her life had recently changed things.

A man, a stranger—an evil, now filling her with a dark dread. She must obey—make him happy—hate, a hatred strong enough to kill.

Inside the room, a flash, a dark shadowy figure, a metal wire around her neck. Horror to all imagined dread, Now inside her home, a murderer has arrived. Reaching back with her right arm and gripping the noose around her neck, Cassia began to fight back against this invader and the wire cutting into her throat.

For now, all she knew was that someone was trying to kill her. Never mind the who, but the why was important. Pushing upward with her legs, she sought to get the upper hand and shoved back against her attacker. As she grunted and groaned, she felt the one behind her move, adjusting their position, never letting go of their deadly grip. This fight to stay alive was unrelenting; she wouldn't go down without a fight.

Next, Cassia felt herself tumbling onto the mattress as she began to choke, the wire cutting off oxygen. She continued her fight to stay alive. Nothing else mattered—not the upcoming vacation plans or the promise that one day she'd have grandchildren. Thoughts, stupid thoughts, flashed in her mind.

Then in the struggle, the ridiculous battle for life, as if a baby was coming into this world, it seemed that she was departing it. As she opened her eyes unexpectedly, there in the dresser mirror, she caught a glimpse of her attacker. The one behind her, choking her to death.

As expected, it was no surprise for her to see the young woman that she had met only a few minutes ago, the very one promising not to be a killer. Now she was dressed all in black and her face was painted white with a facial expression outlined in black, wearing a frown upon her face and looking ridiculous. A street mime, by all accounts

A harsh reality struck her in her bedroom, upon her bed, the place she foretold where she would meet her end. Why her? They'd never met. But regardless, this was it—the curtain was falling, and there would be no more performances. This place was it—no more song, no more sunsets. There in the mirror, gritting her teeth, was the bitch out to kill her dead.

Why is she out to kill me? At least this much I'd like to appreciate, wait, understand. Why this girl, why her? Nonetheless, the metal wire was performing beautifully, and soon the room was darkening, harder to resist, now more than ever.

The girl, this little tramp, who was she? Perhaps the last bit of oxygen stored in the recesses of her brain made her ponder the question, regardless of the deliberation. The one wanting her dead—killing her now—was for the love of the man she'd met some time ago. She had prophesied that the strangler was in love, a sick-minded love. This woman was his lover! Now on her bed, she foretold her future, regardless of what she predicted.

Slowly, all around her, Cassia could barely hear the strenuous panting from her assailant. As a result, the room around her faded into nothingness. But unpredictably, other voices and screams burst into the room.

Next, a single earsplitting gunshot rang out. Everything went black.

Chapter 18

So much blood. The trail was left behind. None could stop it from spilling onto the asphalt—tears and crying, asking forgiveness for disappointing him, the one that meant so much.

"Hush, please don't speak. We're almost free."

Now feeling safe and wrapped in her lover's embrace with his strong arms supporting her, Bridget continued apologizing.

"I only wanted to make you proud, to show you I could kill like you. I never suspected the daughter and her friend with the gun would appear. I had the fortune teller in my grip. But, my love, I'm sorry she got away."

"Don't speak, my love. You little fool, you were only supposed to act the part of the victim. I never intended on you killing her. That was my doing."

"I'm sorry, my darling. I'm afraid our love song will soon be over."

Coughing up blood, more blood, Bridget asked for a kiss, a long goodbye, before departing this world. She knew she could never be saved; she barely escaped as it was. But she was determined to see Harland one last time before dying. She had beat the odds, made her escape, and found him waiting for her.

It was doubtful they would give chase, the ones who saved the lady fortune teller, not knowing where Bridget's lover was hiding. It was more important to them to protect the old lady.

Bridget didn't want to move but was being carried away. The narrow alleys were a blur. The cold penetrated her body. The pain, the deep pain within her chest, somehow all of it was fading. It was no longer hurting as it once did. Now in these last moments of life, she felt content.

Bridget's part in killing her sister and the attempted murder of this stupid fortune teller would never be brought to justice. No, none of it mattered; she soon would be dead.

That day when she first met Harland, she found something about him intriguing. Perhaps she was drawn to his mystery. At first, she was hesitant to kill. But hearing him describe the details and fulfillment she would experience made it all seem appealing. But taking pig blood and coating the women's dirty underwear seemed over the top.

Yes, of course, there was her stepsister who took everything from her. But, with Harland's help, she was soon dealt with. She only intended to return the favor by killing this foolish lady. But she failed in her attempt.

She coughed up more blood, and the last seconds of her life drained as if sand in an hourglass.

Looking up at Harland, Bridget said, "My love, please lay me down somewhere. It doesn't matter if the authorities find me. I'm a goner."

"I'm searching for someplace out of the rain."

"There's no time. I want to kiss you before I go."

Desperately, he looked about and saw the public library was ahead, across the street. Hurrying across the street, Harland rushed up the stairs and burst through the doors. After a quick search, he saw a maintenance closet in the corner. Ignoring the weird stares, he rushed inside. Laying Bridget across an old wooden desk, he grabbed ahold of some dirty coveralls, bundled them into a ball, and placed them under her head.

As he stared at Bridget, a sharp, piercing pain entered his heart. The girl who meant so much, the only one who could remove his deep-seated hate, was now close to death. She no longer spoke, her blank stares drilling into his soul.

"I love you," he said. "Please don't leave me. Please don't leave me alone—not now when we had hoped to get away from the city and leave it all behind us."

Reaching down, he kissed her passionately, ignoring the taste of blood on his lips. As he pulled away, there was a last exhale from her body, then she was gone.

The harsh reality struck him, and he looked up and screamed, "No, no. Don't leave me."

The door to the maintenance closet creaked open, and an old woman called out, "Hello, are you all right, sir?"

Quickly covering his face, Harland pushed past her and ran out of the library into the night.

Almost immediately, the police were called and found Bridget's body—although her assailant was never discovered.

Sometime later, after giving an interview to the detective and the FBI agents, Cassia did her best to describe both the girl who tried to kill her and the stranger whom she saw some months ago. To her, the murderous pair must have selected their victims randomly, although the man must have said something to the girl, speaking of his reason for wanting Cassia dead.

Later while the crime investigators searched for clues, to everyone's amazement, they found a note taped to the crystal ball used in Cassia's fortune telling. The note read:

Dear Someone,

I realize we just met. You probably think this is weird. Regardless of your sentiments, today, you die. If you could tell the future, you would know the reason why.
Signed,
Death Incarnate

Months later, standing alone atop a tall building, a lone figure eyed the city below. The shining lights reflecting off the busy streets below and the drizzling rain combined gave little comfort. When he was a child, the sights and sounds reminded him of Christmas and how he and his sister would share stories of what they hoped to receive from Santa.

Sadly, that was just a fairytale. Life, it seems, had lessons that neither he nor his sister ever expected—one of which was that love so quickly appears and is dashed upon the rocks of despair.

No longer would he make that mistake. No, for him, his next target was hurrying to her car. Try as she might avoid her date with destiny. There was no escape from him. The same could be said about the fortune teller who should have died that day, not Bridget.

Still, time passes, and we get lackadaisical in our lives while time has a way of making us forget. But he will never forget his oath of vengeance until his last dying breath: Harland, the Jackal.

Acknowledgments

I want to thank a wonderful woman named Kristen from Kristen Corrects. She has done a magnificent job of editing this book. So that you, the reader, can follow the story and be intrigued.

Also, Mat from M.Y. Cover Design, whose imagination has proven to be as creative as my writing, together, a world of possibilities exists.

About the Author

Timothy Patrick Means was raised on the sunny beaches of Southern California. He spent many summers swimming and playing in the ocean as a young boy. Later he was fortunate enough to land a job in aerospace, working for McDonnell Douglas. He worked on military aircraft and, most exciting of all, rockets! He learned about all types of space hardware, including the space station, the space shuttle, and the Delta rocket.

His life has always been interesting—a father to four children and two stepchildren, a grandfather to fourteen. And through it all, he has always found time to write. "My first experience at being creative was describing my feelings through poetry, which I did with mixed results," he explains. But it wasn't until he discovered the fun of writing about the paranormal that his imagination soared, and he "was set free to explore all the possibilities of creating an exciting story."

Dear Someone is a standalone novel. Check out his two other series, The Bishops' Sacrifice and The Iron Born Pirates, on Amazon or wherever books are sold. Find out more about him at his website:

www.timothypatrickmeans.com.

Printed in Great Britain
by Amazon